Where Shadows Rise

AMY LAURENS

OTHER WORKS

SANCTUARY

Where Shadows Rise
On Roads Between
When Worlds Collide

Where Shadows Rise

AMY LAURENS

AUSTRALIA

ISBN: 978-0-9945238-6-0

www.inkprintpress.com

National Library of Australia Cataloguing-in-Publication Data
Laurens, Amy 1985 –
Where Shadows Rise
278 p.
ISBN: 978-0-9945238-6-0
Inkprint Press, Canberra, Australia
      1. Fantasy Fiction 2. Fairies 3. Shadows 4. Juvenile
      Fiction

Summary: Edge must figure out what's causing the horrifying
shadows to leak from fairyland in order to save her best friend
(and dog).

First Edition: May 2017
Printed in the United States of America.

Cover design © The Cover Collection.

Loupy, you know this one's always been for you.
(Sorry it took so long!)

1

THE DOORBELL RANG. That doesn't sound exciting in and of itself, but let me assure you: it was the most heart-pounding thing to happen all week. It was my birthday, I was home alone, and because of the stupid witness protection business, I'd been stuck in the house all summer. I hadn't even been allowed out to see friends, because we'd arrived in town at the end of last year with only three school weeks to go—so I didn't have any friends.

Well. I had friends, but they were back in Melbourne, and I wasn't allowed to contact them for fear someone would track down our new location. Lucky me.

Anyway, it was my birthday, I was alone because Mum and Dad had gone to do something regarding birthday surprises and Anna had inexplicably chosen to go with them, and the doorbell had just rung. I stared at the closed door, heart pounding, while our chocolate Labrador, Veve, tried to chew it down. Was I going to open it?

Of course I was going to open it. The chances of it being a mobster were slim to none; for starters, a mobster wouldn't have rung the bell.

I opened it.

"Miss Tanning?" The deliveryman raised a questioning eyebrow and cocked a digital pen at me.

I nodded, heart flip-flopping, and scrawled a fair impersonation of my signature on the digital pad.

He handed over a small, brown-paper parcel with a handwritten address, and departed.

I closed the door behind him, throat dry, and stared down at Veve. On the one hand, yay birthday present. On the other, holy crap, someone had our address. That was *not* a good thing.

It became even less of a good thing when I noticed that the parcel was indeed addressed to a Miss Tanning: a Miss *Anna* Tanning, as in my sister, not me, Emma Tanning.

Anger bubbled up in my chest, hot and tight, and the parcel protested in my grip.

Veve whined softly.

"How could she *do* this?" I whispered to Veve.

I turned the parcel over. It was from Kade, Anna's frogging ex-boyfriend. Who apparently wasn't an 'ex' after all.

Urgh. I ground my teeth. "You know what?" I asked Veve.

She looked up at me with her liquid brown eyes, tongue lolling as she smiled.

"Screw it. If Anna can get interstate mail from people who aren't even supposed to know we exist anymore, you and I can go for a walk on my birthday. What do you think?"

They say dogs don't speak English, but Veve sure as heck knew the word 'walk'—though I think in her vocabulary it was something closer to 'Magical Trip To Disneyland' and less like 'Comparatively Bland Meander Through Trees'. She tucked her tail right under her butt and shot down the hall, whirling in frantic circles a few times at the end before pelting back as I retrieved her lead from the drawer in the front cabinet.

I rolled my eyes as I clipped her lead onto her collar. For my troubles, I got slimed right up the nostrils. "You're disgusting, you know that?" I wiped off the worst of the dog slobber on the shoulder of my shirt. She just grinned.

Out on the street, she leapt and twisted madly. "Hair-brain," I told her, snapping the lead to get her attention. "It's just a walk."

She just snorted—and stiffened. I followed her gaze to where a flock of corellas pecked their way through the dry grass at the end of the street.

"Veve!"

My shout was in vain: the lead burned through my fingers and Veve shot down the road, a chocolate bullet howling death and destruction for all things feathered.

I cursed her to the lower circles of doggie hell. Which probably involved, I don't know, a world devoid of birds, cats, people, sunshine, and walks, if Veve was anything to go by.

"Veve!" If the sight of the mad Lab-rat barrelling toward them hadn't scared the birds off, my shouts would have. "Come back here *now*!"

Predictably, she ignored me, pounding down the slope, through the fringe of gum trees, and down the narrow stairs between giant granite boulders that led to the river.

"Stupid frogging brainless beast of a stupid frogging dog," I muttered as I followed. "If Mum gets home before we do and freaks out, I swear, I'll pluck your tail hairs out."

Empty threats, obviously, but Mum's freak-out wouldn't be. Her thoughts would go straight to the day Anna nearly died—and I wouldn't blame her. I should have left a note. Urgh.

The stairs ended and I found myself on a track broad enough for two twisting along a creek the colour of bitter tea. Tussock grass clustered in spikes—where the eucalypts would let it—and hot summer sunlight glinted from the leaves. Somewhere to my right, downstream and in the opposite direction to the house, Veve barked. I exhaled like a whale coming up for air and set out after her.

Veve bounded out from the undergrowth in front of me, a dolphin leaping through water, tongue flapping with every bound. "Stupid mutt," I told her under my breath.

She didn't care what I thought (of course), and saved a leap for the last minute so she could plant muddy feet on my hips as I tried to catch her collar.

I straightened, about to insult her some more, and realised that she'd gone stiff again, ears pricked and mouth tight, listening down the path.

My neck prickled. Someone was coming. A second later, I heard footsteps in the gravel, and a low, male voice, humming, or maybe singing softly.

My chest constricted, and just as suddenly my hands were slick. Chances were it was just a stranger out for a midday stroll, but my stomach wound knots about my memories and I smelled the hot concrete and melting asphalt, old oil and stale urine of the Lilydale train station where the body had been hidden in a toilet stall, the body of the girl who'd looked like Anna.

I had to get off the path.

"Come on, Veve," I said, pulling her close, white-knuckled as I stepped into the undergrowth. The tea tree scrub protested, but I shoved my way through anyway, glancing over my shoulder as the humming grew louder.

I kept going until I couldn't hear footsteps any more, until the wind swallowed the hum that sounded too like the warning cry of a hive—danger, we're working here, come close and get stung.

I didn't want to get stung; visions of a blood-streaked face refused to be blinked away. Only Veve tugging brought me back to myself, and I realised firstly that I was holding the lead way too tight, cutting off Veve's air supply, secondly that the reason my cheeks were suddenly cold was because I'd been crying, and thirdly that I'd found the creek again, looping back parallel maybe fifty meters or so from the path.

Abruptly, I dropped Veve's lead and strode forward to kneel by the water. I dipped my hands in. A shiver slide through me at its chill, and I scooped it up to wash my face.

Flinging the excess water away, I gulped at the air, deep, calming breaths all the way down into my belly, and visualised a river washing away the blood from my thoughts, just like the police psych had taught me.

Once the space behind my eyes was calm and black, I drew in one last forceful breath, and opened my eyes. Perched on a rock by the creek, I hugged my knees to my chest as cool water lapped at my toes. Veve was a little upstream, just before the creek bent back toward the path, doggy paddling in circles in a deep spot where the water broadened to maybe ten meters across. In front of me it was broad but shallow, only ankle deep, its path torn to white foam by the rocks.

And—I gasped. In the middle of the stream, glittering in the sun like a piece of fallen sky, was the hugest butterfly I'd ever seen. Which was pretty huge; besides the fact that I grew up visiting the Melbourne Zoo with its impressive butterfly house every Christmas since I could remember, Mum and Dad had taken us up to Brisbane for a family holiday two years ago, and we'd seen giant tropical butterflies bigger than my hand.

This one, bright blue with black edging like a Ulysses, was bigger than both my hands put together.

And then it turned around.

Okay. I'd grown up reading fairy tales as much as the next person, and although I'd had a horse-crazy stage instead of a fairy-crazy stage like Anna had, I'd seen all her paraphernalia. Still, none of it prepared me for finding something that looked exactly like a fairy, standing smack in the middle of a creek in boring, backwater Nowra. I'm pretty sure my eyes were only hanging in their sockets by a thread.

And then it talked.

Her face lit up like a cloud had just uncovered the sun as she spotted me. "Hi there!" she said, fluttering over.

I just stared, heart pounding against my ribcage as though it wanted to run away from the absurdity of it all. "No," I said. "I'm hallucinating."

The fairy frowned. "I don't think so."

I shook my head. "No. No, things like this do not happen. Things like this aren't *real*." I stood, backing up a step.

The fairy sighed. "I promise. I'm quite real."

"You would say that, wouldn't you," I said, eyeing her. "Veve!" I waved at the dog and hopped from one foot to the other, trying to lure her in with the promise of play. "We're going now!"

Veve, adorable beast that she was, landed a little upstream and shook vigorously before trotting toward me. I backed hurriedly away from the bank, dancing to keep Veve's attention.

"Wait!" the fairy cried, wings snapping out and propelling her a couple of feet into the air. "You're a Traveller! I need to talk to you!"

"Uh huh, sure," I said as I wound the lead around my hand and set off back into the bushes. This was punishment for leaving the house, obviously. The universe was out to get me, reminding me forcefully that once you started disregarding some rules, who knew what other rules you'd end up flouting.

The rules of physics, for example.

I glanced back once, right before the bushes hid the stream altogether. Blue flashed, high up, but I ducked to get a better view and it was only the sky. I scowled. Stupid fairy. Stupid universe. Served me right for leaving the house in the first place. Urgh. "Come on, Veve," I said, snapping the lead. "Even if the house is prison, at least it's *sane*."

I was stomping so furiously as I burst out onto the path that when a figure rose from a stoop only a couple of steps away, I squeaked in surprise.

I scowled. People rarely surprised me; usually I could tell without trying that someone was near. I really must have been off in my own little world.

I glowered at the boy who lived to make my school life a misery. "What are you doing here?" I snapped. "Isn't it bad enough that I have to deal with you on school days? Which, by the way, don't start until tomorrow. You're ruining my holidays."

Okay, so maybe that was a little harsh, but come on. It was *Scott*. I'd arrived in town with three weeks left in the school year, and he'd spent every day of them humiliating me in front of his mates, and I didn't care for a repeat this year.

Scott eyed me warily, which was a strange expression on him. Usually he strode around like he knew without a doubt that he was too good for the world, and also—somewhere deeper, somewhere I'd only caught a glimpse of once or twice—that it had nothing left to throw at him that could hurt.

Occasionally, in my more generous moments, I wondered what had happened to make him look that way. Mostly, however, I just wondered why he was such a moron.

"What are you doing here?" he asked, voice dripping with accusation and suspicion.

My hands fisted of their own accord, and beside me Veve's hackles rose as she chimed in with a low-pitched, rumbling growl. I flicked the free end of the lead at her nose. "Nothing," I said, in a rousing blaze of wit. "What are you doing?"

He scowled. "You shouldn't be here."

For one heart-stopping instant I thought he meant out here generally, walking around, as if he knew what had happened and why I'd hidden away all summer. Then I realised he was nodding into the undergrowth. I rolled my eyes. "I might be a city slicker," I bit off, "but I'm not stupid. I made enough noise to scare off a herd of elephants, let alone any snakes that might have been lying around." The thought chilled me, though; I *hadn't* been thinking about snakes when I'd hurried off the path. One badly-timed footstep and a brown snake bite later, and I could be a dead body too.

But Scott had moved on, stalking off down the path. He had nice shoulders, I'd give him that much. Pity he couldn't derive his personality from them, instead of whatever dead weight it was he kept inside his head for brains.

Beside me, Veve growled again, louder this time, more urgent. I snapped the lead at her and stared after Scott's retreating form, trying to think of something cutting.

It was only when Veve growled for the third time that I realised she wasn't even facing Scott. Instead, she was looking back into the bushes—and something dark was flickering in there, deep in the shadows of the trees.

My chest squeezed in on itself and adrenalin shot through my body. Veve's growling grew louder until it broke in a bark, something midway between slavering and terrified, and I realised my tongue was stuck to the roof of my mouth. Carefully I peeled it away, unable to tear my eyes from the shifting darkness in the bushes. There was no discernible form, just shadow, darker than it should have been this soon after midday, and a pervasive sense of dread clamping down on me like an on-coming storm.

Veve began backing away, hackles prickling, growl rising and falling like thunder. I glanced down at her, back to the shadows—and they were closer, much closer than they had been.

I turned and bolted.

2

THE BUS PULLED up at school and I wondered if anyone would notice if I didn't get off. My roll call teacher, probably. Maybe. And then Mum when the school called later on to find out why I wasn't there.

I sighed and schlepped off the bus amidst the horde of student clones. Yesterday hadn't ended terribly; I'd been grounded for going out without permission, but as Anna had pointed out, grounding was hardly that much different to witness protection anyway. Plus, unlike Anna, I never broke rules, so Mum had pretty much forgiven me by dinner. We'd had cake and candles and curled up to watch a movie as a family, which was pretty cool. We hadn't done that in... a while. A long while.

But I was still having trouble deciding whether school was better or worse than being cooped up in the house. On the one hand, yay, no house. On the other... I surveyed the unkempt masses between me and my locker and sighed again.

It wasn't their fault. Not really. They had no idea that having travelled to Sydney 'that one time, for Christmas, with my parents' didn't amount to worldly wisdom, or that there were more important things in life than who had dumped who for other-who—like the fact that both whos were still alive, for instance.

I rubbed my hands over my forehead, set my shoulders, and marched on in. I'd survived nearly a month of school here at the end of last year, so I could survive this year.

Semester. Term. Okay, I could definitely at least survive the week.

As I entered H block and headed toward my locker, I downgraded that to 'day': Scott lounged against the lockers like some sort of drug lord (cue involuntary shudder) and eyed me as I approached. He was back in usual form, black hipster-glasses perched precariously on his perfectly-sculpted nose, blond hair gel-spiked to bedhead precision, tie-knot strategically loosened. Greeeat. Here we went again.

"Well hello there, Emma." Eyelash flutter that shouldn't look that natural on a guy, quirk of the perfectly sculpted eyebrow, fold of the arms across the chest. I knew those plays off by heart, thanks to that month last year.

"Scott, you're spreading your germs all over my locker. Move."

His eyebrows jumped suggestively. "Or what?"

"Or I'll go and get Mrs Johnston and have you explain to her why I couldn't access my books." Somehow he'd gotten it into his head that because I didn't immediately bow down and fawn over him when I'd arrived last year, he was in love with me. I would actually rather date dirt, but he just wouldn't take a hint. Or a clue-by-four to the head.

He leered some more. Seriously. It was like he *wanted* me to hit him. "Naw, you wouldn't do that."

I swung my bag off my shoulders and onto the floor at the foot of the lockers—and, somewhat coincidentally, the foot of Scott.

He winced. "Jeez woman, what are you carrying? Bricks?"

"Just for you." I smiled sweetly. "Move."

He looked like he was going to argue some more, but then an arm caught me around the shoulders and the fight went out of his eyes.

Gemma, now draped around my neck, beamed at Scott. "You were just leaving, were you?"

He scowled and disappeared.

I shrugged out of Gemma's half-hug and dove at my locker. "Thanks," I muttered.

Gemma was... Well, Gemma was also arrogant, but not like Scott. With Scott, you knew he thought you were beneath him. With Gemma, she just kind of forgot that other people had feelings that sometimes differed from her own. Her parents had money, and although I wouldn't go so far as to call her spoiled, she did kind of assume the world would revolve around her, lacking any evidence to the contrary. Rules were optional, not because she was naughty, but because she forgot that other people's rules weren't identical to hers.

I didn't like breaking the rules—any rules— because that kind of attitude got you killed. But hey. She was better than Scott, and I supposed she was also better than spending the next school year as a loner.

After stashing my bag and retrieving my books, I let Gemma shepherd me down the hall to roll call, and then when the bell rang ten minutes later, off to science.

"I checked your timetable this morning," she bubbled at me as we wove through the crowd. "We have all our core classes together. Isn't that awesome?"

"Of course we do," I muttered, before correcting myself: "I mean, of course it is. Yay." I managed some semi-enthusiastic jazz hands and a half-hearted smile.

We entered the science classroom and I hesitated for a moment. Gemma usually sat up the back somewhere; I was a front row kinda gal, and I wasn't about to change that for anybody.

Oh well. Sitting by myself wouldn't be *so* bad. I plunked into a front-and-centre seat and arranged my books at neat right angles along the front of my desk, placing a pen and perfectly-sharpened pencil atop them. Gemma pulled out the chair to my left and shot me a sunny smile. Tension I hadn't known was there melted from my shoulders, and I dared a tiny smile in return.

The back of my neck prickled, erasing my half-hearted smile. Cold, vast emptiness niggled at my consciousness, and I knew without looking that Scott would be standing in the doorway, surveying his domain. I stiffened, fighting the urge to turn around. Instead, I pretended to drop my pen on the floor, sneaking a glance under my arm as I bent to pick it up.

Yup, Scott. Oy. As he swept into the room girls paused in their conversations, straightening to emphasise their curves, eyes wide through luxurious curtains of hair.

Okay, okay: the entire room didn't stop just to watch him enter, but the way he walked you'd think the crowd would start offering him babies to kiss any moment now. And at least five of the girls up the back had major crushes on him, so they definitely did the stop-straighten-peer-through-hair thing.

Scott, of course, ignored them, heading straight for me. I wondered why for a brief moment as I replaced my pen on my neat stack of books, and then I realised: the only empty desk was right next to me. *Oh for crying out loud, Universe. Seriously?* I face-planted on the desk, wondering if thinking hard enough would let me melt straight through it and into oblivion.

"We meet again, Emma-my-love."

"Scott," I mumbled at the desk, "what have I ever done to deserve your unwavering attention?" He dropped into the desk to my left. "Please, tell me so I can stop."

"Miss Tanning." I snapped upright at the sound of Mrs Johnston's voice. "If you're quite ready."

I blushed. "Sorry."

Beside me, Scott snickered.

"Shut up," I whispered furiously. "I hate you."

"I'm wounded," he said, putting a hand dramatically to his chest. "What do I have to do to get you to like me?"

"Drop dead?" I offered as chills ran up and down my spine. Something about him really gave me the creeps, and my 'drop dead' suggestion was only *ninety* percent joking.

"Couldn't do that," he chirped. "Then you'd have to live with my death on your conscience, and I know you could never cope with that. Far too high and mighty."

"What?" I lowered my inappropriately loud volume mid-word and cut sharp eyes over to where

Mrs Johnston was handing out worksheets on the other side of the classroom. "I am not high and mighty!" I muttered furiously at Scott. "How dare you judge me! You have no idea about my life!"

A worksheet slapped down on my desk, and I glanced up at Mrs Johnston's disapproving face. "On task," she said. "Now. If you think I'm not willing to hand out detentions in period one on the first day, you're wrong."

Frustration welled up as tears, and I blinked firmly. "Yes, Miss. I'm sorry, Miss."

"Mm." She pursed her lips before moving on.

Scott leaned over just long enough to whisper, "Maybe you shouldn't be the one judging me."

The rest of the day had passed with far less stress—turned out I only had to deal with Scott in science, maths and English—and no more disapproval from teachers, thank goodness.

After dinner I lay sprawled on my bed, in theory going through the snowdrift of paperwork I'd accumulated during the day, but actually just staring out my window. If my subconscious was going to magic something up to personify the anxiety I'd been having since the girl—Georgia, her name was Georgia, and the psych had told me that even though saying her name felt uncomfortable, it would help me process it faster—since *Georgia* had been murdered, then I could understand that. After all, it had thrown vivid nightmares at me every night for two months afterwards. It had been about a month since the nightmares had ceased, so probably I was due for some kind of relapse.

But why a fairy? That's what was really getting to me. The shadows I could understand: a vague, dark menace that I couldn't control, approaching from the shadows around me... That made sense. But a fairy? Seriously? I couldn't even begin to imagine what that might mean.

Idly, I punched holes in the paperwork and slid it all into my tabbed and colour-coded folder. Shadows made *sense*. A fairy was just bizarre.

A tap on my door interrupted my thoughts. I shook them away. "Come in, Anna."

She stuck her head into my room. "Hey, Edge," she said, using the nickname we'd made out of my initials, E. J. "How was day one?"

I shrugged. "Fine. I'm filing," I said, lifting papers as proof.

Anna rolled her eyes. "You are way too organised to be human, you know. It isn't normal."

I shrugged again. "Sure. How was your day?"

She grinned. "Oh, you know. The usual."

I raised a sceptical eyebrow. "Seriously? Day one and you were in the principal's office already? What did you do, strip naked in the quad?" It couldn't have been *that* bad; I'd have heard something if the school's newest year twelve student had done something *really* stupid on the first day back.

It was Anna's turn to shrug as she stepped into my room and closed the door behind her. "Actually I just wanted to ask about changing out of art."

"Really?" Both my eyebrows lifted this time. "But you know it's too late to change subjects."

She scowled. "Thus have I been informed. It's stupid. I had literally five minutes to choose my subjects when we arrived last year, and art's ridiculous; Mr Ridely's a joke. It's a complete waste of time, and I'm awful at it, and I wish they'd just let me switch out and be done with it." She slumped against the wall, arms folded tightly across her chest.

"Sorry," I said, shifting uncomfortably on my bed. "That's the system for you."

"Yeah, well, this system sucks."

"Yeah." It did kind of suck that we couldn't have at least stayed in the same state, but those were the rules we'd been given, and we had to stick to them.

Cogs turned. Fairies and rules, Anna and her stuff-the-rules attitude... I licked my lips. "Anna? Can I... Can I ask you something weird?"

She cocked her head. "Sure. Hit me."

My mouth felt suddenly dry. I swallowed a couple of times, heart racing as I tried to figure out how to verbalise my thoughts. "I... I mean you..." I took a deep breath and told myself to stop being stupid. "Why don't you care about the rules? Like, ever?"

Anger flashed in her eyes as she drew herself upright, and I hurried to forestall it.

"I'm not talk about the g—about Georgia. I mean generally. All the time. You never seem to care about what other people think or what you're meant to be doing and I don't get it. I'm just trying to understand, I promise, I'm not judging you. I just wondered..." *How you live with yourself. Why you're not the one seeing fairies. Are you seeing fairies? Anna, do you have hallucinations?*

I shook my head. "I don't even know what I'm asking. Sorry." I went back to my hole punching.

Anna eyed me thoughtfully—I could feel the weight of her strawberries-and-cream gaze out of the corner of my eye, hear the tiny clack-clack-clack of spider feet that I'd learned to associate with her thinking—then abruptly sank to the floor. She rubbed at the back of her neck and seemed to be searching for words.

"I don't know," she said in the end. "I'm not like you, or Mum, or even Dad. You guys just... It's easy, for you," she continued. "I mean, look at you. It's the first day of school and you're already doing homework, organising your notes within an inch of their lives. I feel claustrophobic just looking at it.

Don't you ever just long for some space, for five minutes where you don't have to worry about doing the right thing and saying the right words, where you can ask questions of the universe and demand answers?"

I flinched away from the conviction of her gaze.

"No," she said more softly. "I guess you don't, any more than I like your rules and plans and organisation." She shrugged. "The universe is full of questions, Edge, and 'just because' is never a good enough answer." She unwound to a stand, long-legged, lithe like a lioness who knew how to hunt what she needed to survive. "How else do you know you're alive?"

Blood, crimson lines on porcelain-white tiles. I knew what she meant, a little. I'd never been so aware of *life* before I'd been confronted so violently by death.

I nodded. "Thanks." My voice was dry and raspy, and I couldn't bring myself to meet her eye.

She nodded back, though—"Welcome."—and disappeared back to the hall.

Shadows drifted down the hallway toward me, filling the doorway of my room like smoke before billowing over the threshold and into my room. I backed up in my bed until I pressed against the cold glass of the window.

A fluttering sort of tap made me turn, and against the window a bright blue bird hopped and scratched, trying to get in. Beyond it, more shadows mounted, frothing forth from underneath the prickly bushes that marched along the fence.

Something cold touched my hand, and I jumped. The bird. The bird had gotten inside, blue like the sky, wings stretched as wide as my two hands together, covered not in feathers but in tiny, iridescent scales—butterfly wings, edged in black.

Shadows slid toward me from my doorway, through the window, and I clutched the fairy tightly. She cried out, and I opened my hand to see nothing but red, a double-handful of sticky, crimson blood on hands so pale they seemed white.

The shadows whispered toward me. *Surrender. Surrender...*

3

I WOKE IN the morning sick and exhausted, vague memories of bad dreams hanging over me. I knew from experience that wallowing around the house all day would only make things worse, so I got up, got ready for school, and headed off on the bus, pretending I didn't twitch whenever I saw darkness in the corners of my vision.

The first two periods passed uneventfully enough—electives, so I had neither Gemma nor Scott to entertain or annoy me respectively—and after recess I had my first appointment with the school counsellor. It went about as well as I'd expected.

Back in the empty halls, I slammed my locker shut and leaned my head against it. The visits to the counsellor were compulsory for now, but I missed the awesome woman the police had assigned me back in Melbourne. I'd only spoken to her twice, but she'd been kind, and understanding, and gentle. The school counsellor was a little more confrontational than I'd have liked.

Okay, a lot more confrontational, and I'd left with a headache and anger bubbling away in my stomach.

"You need to let go, Emma," I mimicked cruelly. She had no freaking idea what she was talking about. I *wanted* to let it go. It wasn't like I *enjoyed* having nightmares and being twitchy and irritable.

"Hey there."

I jumped, bashing my elbow against the sharp metal corner of the locker. "Go away, Scott," I said, blinking furiously and hoping he wouldn't see the glistening on my cheeks.

He hesitated and out of the corner of my eye I saw his jaw working. "Are you okay?"

I closed my eyes and slumped forward against the locker. "Brilliant." A sudden sob forced its way through my throat.

Scott paused awkwardly, then put a hand on my shoulder. I tensed, cold seeping into my body. "Hey," he said softly. "It's okay."

I shrugged his hand forcibly away from me and glared. "No, Scott, it's not okay. Nothing is okay. I left my friends, my home, my *life*..." I trailed off as tears choked my words. I couldn't even *begin* to describe the nightmares of blood and shadow—not that I was supposed to mention them. As far as everyone here knew, we'd moved for Mum and Dad's work.

The bell rang.

Scott's lips twitched and I thought for a split second that he might speak again, and that it might even be something nice—and then the crowds poured out of the classrooms and he stiffened.

"Ooo, Scott and Emma, sitting in a tree," a boy taunted as he wandered past.

"Shut up, Mitch," Scott muttered, shooting him a look.

Mitch just grinned. "Aw, you know you wish it was true." He punched Scott's arm and hurried off.

It took me a second to recognise the half-concealed expression on Scott's face as embarrassment, and I softened a little.

Then he smirked, and my stomach dropped. "So Emma," he said far too loudly. "Finished crying over your old school yet?"

The blood drained from my face. "I hate you," I said tightly.

"I know you don't." Scott grinned, showing too much tooth. "Hey guys!" he called to the pack of derelicts he called friends. "Emma said she *loooves* me!"

His mates hollered and cheered.

I wanted to sink through the floor. Or smash him in the face. Or maybe both, in reverse order.

Instead I spun away and tore my locker door open just for the satisfaction of hearing it clang. "I hate you, Scott Harden," I said furiously, not caring whether he heard me or not. "Don't ever come near me again."

A hand on my shoulder made me whirl back again, ready to punch him in the face—but it was Gemma, wide-eyed with concern. "You okay?"

"Brilliant," I snapped, tearing books from my locker like they'd personally offended me.

"Do you want to skip class and talk about it?"

I blinked. "Um, no?"

Gemma laughed, withdrawing her hand. "Wow, okay, it was just a suggestion. It's not like we'd miss much you know, and I doubt we'd even get into trouble."

I shook my head. "No. I'm fine." I gathered up my books and shut the locker. "Class is good." I tried for a smile that felt thin and brittle.

Gemma laughed again and tucked her arm through mine. "Fine. Well, I know something we can talk about to cheer you up."

I quirked a sceptical eyebrow at her. "Mm?"

She grinned. "The fact that I'm going to call you Jeanette for the rest of your life unless you offer me an alternative."

I stopped in my tracks, part playing along, part genuinely horrified. "You wouldn't." Jeanette, my middle name, had come from a great aunt who'd died not long before I'd been born. She'd probably been a lovely person and all, but I detested the name. *How* had Gemma found out my middle name? I shook my head and carried on walking. "What's wrong with Emma anyway?"

Gemma leaned her head awkwardly on my shoulder. "Because, dearest BFF of mine, it's far too close to Gemma. People will get us confused."

I took a moment to absorb that. On the right, Gemma, dark-haired, brown-skinned, beautiful and sparkly and confident of her place in the world. On the left... Well, me. Mousy hair, averagely tanned skin, and nondescript, still carrying a little baby fat around my hips and face—easy to ignore, made more for blending into the background than standing out in a crowd.

I sighed at the thought of anyone ever getting us confused. "I highly doubt that, Gemma."

"Gem," she responded brightly.

"What?"

"Gem! My nickname is Gem! Because you can't make anything else out of Gemma but Ma, and Ma is stupid. But it still doesn't resolve our problem, because Em is the obvious choice for Emma, and Gem and Em might as well be Gemma and Emma." She drew my arm to her side. "So, you know, unless you offer something else, I'll call you Jeanette."

I could tell by the wicked edge to her grin that she knew exactly what kind of a threat that was.

Man *alive* but I'd love to know where she got her information. I exhaled dramatically as we reached the classroom, secretly grateful for the distraction.

"Edge," I pronounced solemnly, peering down my nose at her. "My name is Edge. It's from my initials," I explained in response to her obvious confusion.

"Ah!" She smiled and pulled my arm tight again, an odd sort of meld between a hug and a claim of ownership. "I like it," she said. "Edge."

I arrived home that afternoon to find Anna waiting for me, which was odd. Anna usually caught the last possible bus out of school so she go ride it looping through the suburbs—an excuse to spend longer with the friends she'd made within about three seconds of arriving last year, and to avoid the house as long as possible.

Today, though, I opened the front door and she bounded up from where she'd been sitting in the family room.

"Oh, you're home, are you," she said, sounding an awful lot like Mum.

I rubbed my forehead. "Anna, I've had a really long, sucky day, so if you have a problem, seriously, take a number."

"One," she said, clipping the word. She flourished a pearlescent envelope under my nose. "What *I'd* like to know," she continued, "is why, having made *such* a big deal about me getting a parcel from Kade, *you* seem to have gone behind all our backs and given out your address to some freak whose name doesn't even make sense!"

I caught Anna's wrist and forced her to hold the envelope still so I could read it. Adrenalin shot through the pit of my stomach: the letter was addressed to me. I snatched it from her and pushed past down the hall. "I have no idea who this is from," I snapped. "And I haven't given our address to anyone."

"Hypocrite," Anna called as I slammed my door. "I'm telling Mum!"

Heart pounding as though I'd run the whole way home, I dumped my school bag, kicked off my shoes, and plonked onto the bed clutching the pearly envelope like death. The front bore my name in big, loopy handwriting—and there was no stamp.

My pulse calmed a little at that; it must have been hand delivered, which meant someone local, rather than a stalker. Unless it was a local stalker. Ha ha.

Hurriedly, I flipped it over and scanned the address. Hmm. I could see what Anna meant. The address read like the definition of obscure: Quoise, The Lodge, Sanctuary.

Sanctuary. Maybe they meant Sanctuary's Point? That was a suburb a little way down the coast from here—too far to walk and a long trip on public transport, but it wasn't *entirely* impossible that someone might have driven over to deliver the letter. It seemed like a lot of effort, though; surely the post would have been easier?

I bit my lip. Fingers trembling, I tore the envelope open and pulled out the most beautiful invitation I'd ever seen. Even my cousin Kelly's wedding invitations hadn't been this fancy.

Thick, pearly cardstock bore silver and gold embossed letters in stunning calligraphy. It took me a moment to remember I was supposed to read the invitation, not just stare at it in awe.

I read it, and stared some more. It had to be a hoax—but who on earth would know I'd hallucinated a fairy down by the creek? No one had been there, and I hadn't said a word about it.

Well, Scott had been there, I remembered, frowning. But surely he hadn't known anything about the fairy. Unless I'd been mumbling about it as Veve and I had reached the track? I didn't think so; if I had been, Scott wouldn't have passed up the opportunity to mock me there and then. And sending an invite like this wasn't his style.

But who then?

I shook my head. It made no sense at all. I tucked the beautiful invitation back into its envelope and hid it between some books before grabbing my maths textbook out of my schoolbag.

But no matter how much I tried to remember what Gemma had explained about algebra, all I could think of was the invitation:

Dear Emma,

It is our great pleasure to inform you that you are a Traveller, able to cross between worlds to Sanctuary, home of the fairies. We would dearly love to introduce you as soon as possible. Please meet your appointed fairy at your nearest crossing on Wednesday at five in the evening.

Kindest regards,

The Keeper,

On behalf of the Sanctuary fairies.

4

I'D SPENT MOST of Thursday distracted by the invitation, alternating between hope and despair— *Maybe it's real! Ridiculous, it's obviously a hoax. There's no such thing as fairies!*

Veve growled at the shadows as well, there was something in there... Rubbish, she was growling at Scott, and even if she wasn't, that's all the more reason not to go back there. Those shadows weren't exactly friendly. Besides. You're still housebound. You couldn't go down even if you wanted.

By the time I got off the bus with just two streets to walk to home, my head was whirling.

Mum greeted me the second I walked in. "How was your day?" she said from the kitchen, knife thudding on a chopping board.

"I survived," I said, kicking my shoes off in the hallway.

"I have some news from the police," Mum said. "But go get changed first."

I headed down to my room, stomach flip-flopping back and forth. Why the police? Mum didn't sound stressed, so it couldn't be *that* bad, but... I squeezed my eyes shut against visions of a blood-stained face. Would her—would *Georgia's* face ever stop haunting me? Urgh.

Out of my uniform, I hurried to the kitchen, snagging an apple from the fruit bowl as I passed and trying to act casual. "So, what's up?"

Mum looked up from the pumpkin she'd been chopping, an odd expression on her face. Puzzled, I slid onto one of the barstools.

"So you had a good day, then?" Mum asked.

"I wouldn't say 'good'," I replied around a mouthful of apple. *Come on, Mum. You're killing me.*

"Ah, well," said Mum, resuming her chopping. "And what's this about you receiving a letter?"

I squirmed. "Oh, it was just a note my friend from school dropped off." Guilt gnawed at me.

"Oh, that's lovely."

Colour me suspicious, but Mum was acting beyond weird. I realised where I knew her expression from—it was exactly the same expression Anna got when she was up to something. Curiouser and curiouser.

Mum set the knife down on the bench. "Well, the police called."

The apple froze halfway to my mouth. "Yes, you said that," I said, trying to contain my impatience.

Her eyes sparkled. "They've arrested someone in connection with the murder."

My stomach flipped. "What?"

"This doesn't mean it's over," she added hurriedly. "The gang was far too well connected for one arrest to make us safe."

My stomach flopped back the other way as I realised Mum's eyes were sparkling because they were filled with unshed tears.

"But it's a start. We still have to be careful—no gallivanting around town by yourself, no widespread sharing of our address, and, I'm sorry to say, no social media still—"

Bah and humbug to that.

"—but at the very least it means you can take Veve for walks around the neighbourhood if you like. Maybe down to the creek, she'd like to swim."

I slipped around the bench to hug Mum. "Thank you," I said, punctuating it with a squeeze.

Mum laughed and hugged me back, wiping at her eyes. "I knew you'd be happy."

Happy didn't begin to cover it. Mum was right. This definitely wasn't an end, but it was a very welcome start. "I'll bet you are too," I said, squeezing her again and breathing in the delicious smell of cookie dough that always seemed to linger around her.

"Of course." She clung to me for a few moments longer before untangling herself. "Anyway, I know you're technically grounded, but I thought, given the circumstances, you might want to celebrate. I hear Veve's itching to get out of the yard." She twitched her eyebrows at me and I laughed.

"Thanks, Mum." I headed out to the hallway to grab some shoes and Veve's lead. "I'll be back for dinner!"

"Take your phone!" Mum called back.

Out in the yard, Veve leapt like a mad fish at the sight of her lead, and I laughed. "We're free, girl! For a little bit, anyway."

I nearly had to sit on her to attach the lead, and her efforts to get me through the gate and down the street were enthusiastic to say the least. By the time we got to the stairs through the boulders, my hand hurt from holding her back. I tugged her to a halt. "Veve, *sit*."

She plonked her butt down next to me, tail wagging furiously, a silly, happy grin on her face.

I rolled my eyes, but if I was being truthful, my face was pretty much a mirror of hers. "All right, beast," I murmured as I unclipped the lead. "Don't run too far, okay?"

Veve tensed, waiting for me to release her, and as soon as I did she pelted down the steps.

I followed, shaking my head. As I reached the bottom I heard the splash of her totally inelegant entry into the stream. Now I just had to hope she wouldn't bounce some poor, unsuspecting stranger with her soggy wet feet. Veve pelted toward me through the trees, spray glittering in the afternoon sunshine. That was one advantage of brown dogs: you couldn't tell the difference between dirty and clean.

I set off up the path, slapping my thigh. "Come on, girl."

She snuffled my hand and bounded away again.

A flock of sparrows erupted into the sky and Veve leapt, trying to follow them. They wheeled away, squeaking angrily at the creature who'd frightened them.

Nerves flushed through my stomach. What if the fairy was real? Would Veve try to chase her like she had the birds? What if Veve caught her?

Nerves piled on top of nerves. I reached the place where we'd turned off the path last time and called Veve back, clipping her lead on just in case. I took a deep breath, heart pounding. What if the fairy wasn't there? What if she *was*?

I shook my head and pushed forward through the bushes. "Here we go," I muttered.

I didn't realise I'd been holding my breath until I emerged at the creek and saw the fairy standing with her back to me, bright blue wings glimmering in the sunlight as she stared at the opposite bank. Relief burst over me and I felt like iron bands around my chest had been cut loose. Not a hallucination. There really was a fairy.

Veve, however, was not relieved. She crouched in front of me, snarling as her hackles rose.

"No, Veve." I yanked sharply on the lead.

The fairy turned, face grave.

Veve barked, a throaty alarm call. Before I could brace myself, she sprang, and I had the familiar sensation of the lead burning through my fingers.

"Genevieve!" I screamed as she hurtled toward the fairy. "No!"

5

VEVE BOUNDED AT the fairy, snarling, and leapt
into the air. The fairy squeaked and ducked, arms
shielding her head. Veve sailed through the air
toward her—and kept on sailing, landing with an
almighty splosh in the creek. Had she completely
misjudged the jump?

But she continued through the creek and up onto
the opposite bank, and I collapsed to my knees in
relief. The fairy and I stared as Veve dashed into the
trees, hackles raised, barking madly.

She disappeared and I gasped—then promptly
fell sideways on the ground, laughing hysterically.
On the one hand, my dog had just disappeared in a
snarling fit. But on the other, she hadn't eaten,
bitten, trampled or otherwise mauled the fairy. And
there was a fairy. A fairy!

The fairy stared after her. "I hope she's okay."

I wiped my eyes and sat up straight. "Why shouldn't she be?" But shivers rippled down my spine. The fairy was real. What did that make the shadows?

The fairy gave the opposite bank one last look before turning to me with a sigh. "I'm not sure. Does she usually come back?"

I frowned. "Of course." The shadows there still seemed thicker than normal, like last time, and the prickly, ominous feeling ran over my skin like oil. "What's she chasing?" I asked.

"How should I know?"

I watched the fairy closely. "You were staring over there when we arrived. I thought you might have seen something."

She glanced across the creek and resettled her wings. "No. I've no idea." Abruptly she fluttered over and perched by my knee. "Are you ready?" Her tone signalled the end of the discussion.

I frowned. Veve would be fine. They were just shadows, right? "I've no idea," I replied. "What am I even here for?"

The fairy laughed, a quicksilver sound like tiny bells. "Yes, you probably have some questions, don't you. First of all, I'm Quoise," she said, offering me her hand.

I reached for it, then stopped, wondering how to deal with the mechanics of shaking a hand the size of my pinkie's tip.

Quoise laughed again and shook my finger. "You're Emma. I found out that much already. But I haven't seen you around before. Are you new?"

Her voice was soothing, and her interest genuine. I smiled. "Yeah. My family just moved up here from Melbourne."

Quoise lifted her eyebrows in surprise. "That's quite a move."

"Heh. You're telling me."

"Okay," she said, settling herself on the ground and rubbing a small area clear of debris. "Let me start at the beginning then. Here." She pulled out something tiny and brown from her pocket, and held it up for me.

I put my palm out flat and she dropped the object onto it. "A seed," I said.

She nodded.

"What do I do with it?"

"First of all, you listen," Quoise said, leaning back on her hands and staring up at me. "What do you know about Sanctuary?"

"Honestly?" I said. "Nothing. I've heard of Sanctuary's Point, but I've never heard of a place called Sanctuary."

Quoise nodded. "That's quite normal. Sanctuary means refuge, you know that, yes? Well our Sanctuary, it's not a place of refuge from anything in particular, but it was created to be a refuge from everything, and from time itself."

"How can somewhere be a refuge from time?" I asked, glancing uneasily at the shadows across the creek. Veve would be back in just a second...

Quoise waved her hand dismissively, recapturing my attention. "That's not important quite yet. All you really need to know is that Sanctuary is a place created for you to use whenever you need it."

Across the other side of the stream, Veve's alarm bark rang out.

Nerves pooled in my stomach and I tensed. The shadows thickened. "Maybe I should go find her," I murmured, half rising.

"No." Quoise's tone froze me in place. "No," she repeated, softer. "I think it's better that you stay on this side of the stream for now."

"But Veve..." I said, gesturing.

Quoise shook her head. "I'll call her in a minute if need be. Listen." She pulled another seed out from her pouch. "Not every person can cross to Sanctuary. People who can are called Travellers, and they usually occur in families, though not always."

I wrenched my gaze back. Veve was a dog in the middle of suburbia, I told myself. She'd be perfectly fine. And Quoise had said she'd get her in a minute if she didn't come back by herself. Veve was perfectly fine. "So how can you tell who's a Traveller and who's not?"

Quoise looked smug. "We're fairies. It's our job to tell."

"Okay, so I'm a Traveller." And maybe also dreaming. "How do I travel to Sanctuary?"

"With a sacrifice," she said.

"A sacrifice?" A dead girl, skin bloody. White tiles, streaked with red.

I must have paled, betraying the direction of my thoughts, because Quoise smiled. "Death or life. Travelling between worlds is a gift, in a way; the world is giving you something by allowing you to travel across the borders, so you should give something back in return."

I nodded. That seemed fair enough. "And we give life...?" I prompted, hoping Quoise would elaborate further.

"Yes." Her wings gave a flap. "*Some* people offer death sacrifices, but death sacrifices will *not* get you into Sanctuary. And anyway,"—she brightened—"I don't think we have to worry about *you* attempting a death sacrifice."

My eyebrows quirked. "Hardly."

She glanced at the other bank again. Had the shadows grown even darker, or was I imagining it? "Ordinarily, I'd walk you through it yourself. But if it's alright, today I'll just give a demonstration."

I nodded and Quoise thrust her seed into the ground, murmuring as she did.

A sharp tingle raced up my spine. Somehow she'd planted the seed deep in the ground without leaving a trace. I stared, awed—and nothing else happened. "That's it?" I said, unable to keep the disappointment from my voice.

Quoise's lips quirked upwards in a fleeting smile. "I need you touching me so we can cross."

"Oh," I said. My gaze drifted to the other side of the creek again. Of course Quoise hadn't done anything yet. She'd wait a second until Veve got back before doing anything else.

A yelp echoed across the stream and I was on my feet in an instant.

"No!" Quoise zoomed up. "You can't!"

"That was Veve," I said. "She's hurt!" I stepped around Quoise.

"Emma, please!" Quoise hovered in front of me again at eye level, staring intently at me. "You have to listen to me. Call her as much as you like, but you *can't go over there.* You're a Traveller. Travellers are *not allowed to go over there.*"

Veve yelped again and I ran to the stream. "Veve!" I yelled. "Veve, come here!" I wanted to plunge to her rescue—but I hesitated on the bank, transfixed by the lurking shadows. I definitely wasn't imagining it. Shadows shouldn't be that dark, not this early in the afternoon, not with the hot sun shining in a clear blue sky. Fear slithered between my shoulder blades and sweat broke out on my palms.

Something tugged my hair and I jumped around, pulse racing.

"You can't—go—over!" Quoise said, punctuating each word with a tug on my hair.

I grabbed her gently. "I'm not!" I said. "I'm not." I set her on my shoulder and turned back toward the opposite bank.

Something rustled through the bushes. "C'mon, Veve!" I called. "Here, girl!"

"Emma, we need to go," Quoise said behind me, voice suddenly fearful. "I know you're worried about Veve, but she's a dog, they're not after—" She cut off abruptly, the kind of full stop that meant she was too afraid to say any more.

I turned to her, hands fisting at my sides. "*Who's* not after dogs?"

"Nothing, that's not what I meant. Please, I think it's really important that we leave *now*." She rubbed at her upper arms, gaze darting to the shadows across the creek and back again.

"I'm not leaving without Veve," I said.

The shadows bulged. Surely they hadn't covered that rock in the stream a second ago.

"Emma, she'll be fine."

I froze, staring at the creeping shadows.

"Emma, I really think it's time to go now."

They crept farther.

"Emma? Emma, please get over here!"

I backed away from the stream, eyes wide, heart in my throat. *Veve.*

"Emma, hurry!"

The shadows deepened, making it hard to see where water ended and bank began. "I can't leave without her," I whispered. But I backed farther away without even meaning to; everything about the shadows shouted at me to run.

Quoise flew into my calf and I glanced down at her frustrated face, surprised to see that I'd reached the little clear patch in the dirt—and that a dandelion now bloomed in the middle of it.

"Emma, we have to leave. Sit down, please!"

Unable to think straight through the fear that licked at my chest, I crouched.

Veve exploded out of the undergrowth on the opposite bank, shattering my terror.

I lunged toward her, jumping a few paces into the stream. "Veve, come here!"

She bounded through the water and leapt at me, shadows flying in her wake.

"Hurry," Quoise called. "Grab her!"

I hauled Veve toward me, wrapping my arms around her neck and diving toward Quoise, reaching her just as the world faded away.

Then there was nothing but blackness, the beating of my heart, and Veve's warm, furry body huff-huff-huffing in my arms.

6

THE WORLD REAPPEARED—or *a* world did, at least. As my pulse slowly calmed, I noted that we'd arrived on lush emerald grass encircled by a white wall, which was broken just ahead by an archway.

Veve struggled out of my arms and slopped her tongue at my cheek. I giggled, and the tension broke.

Quoise laughed too. Veve turned to her, ears pricked and nostrils flaring gently as she sniffed.

I tightened my grip on her collar just in case, but instead she whuffed in delight and gave Quoise a slop of approval as well, covering her head-to-toe in drool.

"Veve!" I jerked her away. "You little snot."

Quoise held up her dripping arms. "Well," she said. "Nice as it is to have the approval of the guard mutt, that was one kiss I could have done without."

I laughed too loudly, sounding slightly hysterical. "What *was* that? The shadows, I mean."

Quoise shook her head. "Nothing." She flew upwards and performed a dazzling series of pirouettes, dog slobber flying off her in gobs and glops. "Come on," she said when she was done, heading for the archway.

I stood, brushing dirt from my knees and butt. "It wasn't nothing," I said. "You were scared. *I* was scared." A gentle glimmer in the grass caught my eye, and I realised a series of domed glass beads ringed the place where we'd been sitting.

"It was nothing," Quoise insisted. "Now come on. I want to show you something."

Right. Clearly discussing the shadows was a no-go. I joined her in the archway.

"This," Quoise said proudly, "is Sanctuary."

A vast meadow of grass lay before me, sloping gently uphill. Dense forest obscured our view to the right, craggy mountains rising above it in the distance. To the left, the trees were softer, sparser, and I caught a hint of water beyond them. Halfway up the slope ahead of us, a slightly ramshackle building perched like a mushroom in the grass. "Our destination," Quoise said, pointing at it before flying off.

As I followed, Quoise galloped off in the direction of the beach. "Will she be safe?" I called, jogging to catch up to Quoise.

Quoise smiled back at me over her shoulder. "Sanctuary, remember? Everything is safe here."

As Veve neared the trees, a flock of crimson and purple birds took flight. She jumped at the trees, barking with body-wriggling enthusiasm.

When the last bird had disappeared, she trotted back to me, head and tail high—because clearly scaring away the terrifying birds was something to be proud of.

"Yeah, good job, Hairbrain," I told her as she approached. "Real impressive."

She upended herself at my feet, tripping me to a halt, and obligingly I rubbed her belly for her.

"Come on," Quoise said. "I want to show you the best bit."

My heart fluttered in anticipation as we headed up the slope, our way lit by Sanctuary's strange, pervasive glow. "Where does the light come from?" I asked as we neared the stables.

"Everywhere," Quoise replied. "And nowhere. It just is."

"There's no sun?" I scanned the sky, which was the indeterminate grey-blue of a sky right before sunrise.

"A sun would mean that we were orbiting a star, which would mean Sanctuary was in the same plane of existence as Earth," Quoise said as she hovered by the stable door.

I blinked. "It's not?"

She laughed. "Well, it wouldn't make a very good sanctuary then, would it?" She twirled in the air. "No. Sanctuary is everywhere and nowhere, a portal to all worlds and all dimensions. You can get to anywhere from Sanctuary."

Wow. This was so not a conversation I'd ever expected to have in actual real life.

But the surprises kept coming: as we neared the little building, a familiar face appeared in the doorway. Adrenalin trilled through my chest. "Gemma?"

Her face split into a grin like the sun from behind a cloud. "Edge! You made it!" She swept me up in her trademark possessive bear hug. "I can't believe you're a Traveller too," she gushed. "Isn't this just the best thing ever?"

I couldn't move. Literally, because Gemma was squashing me tight, but also out of shock: fairies were real. Fairy *land* was real. I could travel there, and so, apparently, could Gemma. "I guess we have to be BFFs now," I said, mostly teasing.

She poked me in the shoulder. "Tragic."

We were still laughing when another fairy fluttered up, this one with wings the colour of blood, edged in silver. "Quoise," the red fairy said. Her tone sobered us in an instant. "I'm so glad you're here. There's something..." Her gaze flickered over Gem and me for just an instant. "I need to talk to you."

Quoise turned to me and smiled brightly—too brightly. "I'm sorry," she said. "I'll just be a minute. You go on inside and see the twins."

"Twins?" I asked. "What twins?"

Quoise's smile relaxed. "You'll see. Head right to the back. I'll join you in a second."

Gem tucked my arm in hers. "Come on. You'll want to see this."

I followed her into the dim building—a stable, the aisle lined with empty stalls. Something moved in the straw down the far end, and I headed over to investigate.

Gem held me back. I shot her a puzzled glance, but she pressed one finger against her lips and tilted her head toward the door. Brow wrinkled, I crouched with her as she lifted the flap of the door a little and peered out.

Over her shoulder I could see Quoise a little way off, conferring quietly with the red fairy. "What's going on?" I whispered.

She shook her head. "Later."

I couldn't hear everything, but the snatches I caught sent shivers down my spine. Shadows, darkness, something changing. That sounded too much like what had happened back in the clearing.

I rubbed goosebumps from my arms. The train station had seemed safe, too. I'd have to be careful.

Gem mustn't have understood any more of the conversation than I did; after only a minute or two she stood abruptly, brushing her pants down and sniffing in disgust. "Later," she insisted, cutting off my questions before they could leave my lips. She strode away down the aisle.

I shrugged. "Come on, Veve," I muttered, and followed.

The main aisle was dim and rather dusty, and I sneezed at the chaff our footsteps stirred. But right at the back, a bit of roof had broken away, allowing a beam of light to filter down and illuminate the largest stall. Gem already leaned over the top rail, ignoring me in preference to watching whatever was in there. I crept up, Veve following just as quietly, and peered over the gate.

I gasped. Lying in the straw were two tiny foals, no bigger than Veve. They glittered like 24-carat gold, and if it hadn't been for the gentle rising and falling of their ribs as they slept, I'd have thought they were statues—an effect enhanced by the tiny, inch-long horns that spiralled out of their foreheads. They felt like peace and happiness, pure contentment and deep, dreamy sleep.

"Aren't they incredible?"

I nodded. I could watch them forever.

Veve snuggled up in the straw at my feet, and I leaned on the gate, staring at the foals. So beautiful.

I'd had a unicorn statue once. The unicorn had been white with a blue mane and tail, and golden hooves. It had been my favourite thing ever—until it had broken when my ex-best friend Grace had volunteered to help clean my room one day.

Quoise fluttered down the aisle and alighted on the railing next to me. Gem shot her a poisonous look and stalked outside.

I hesitated. Should I follow Gem, or stay here with Quoise?

"Lovely, aren't they?" said Quoise.

"Where's their mother?" Gem would be okay by herself for a minute, and maybe I could find out what Quoise had been talking about. That would probably make Gem happier.

Quoise perched on the gate. "We're not sure."

I glanced at her worried face. "That doesn't sound good."

"It's not. Usually you couldn't pry a unicorn mother away from her babies for all the love in the world." Quoise shrugged. "We haven't heard any bad news, though. Everyone's on the lookout," she added softly. "No news is good news, right?"

I nodded, wanting to reassure her, but inside I writhed. *No. Sometimes no news means that someone's too dead to call home.*

"Sanctuary's..." I adjusted my grip on the railing. "I mean, this is a good place, right? It's safe?"

"Of course it's safe," Quoise said firmly. "I told you that."

I nodded and cast around for a new topic. "So, are you good friends with the red fairy?"

"Ruby?" Quoise's eyebrows lifted in surprise. "I suppose so. Why?"

I shrugged. "You two come here a lot, is all. I was wondering if you came together or separately."

Quoise furrowed her brow. "How do you know we come here at all?"

I shrugged again. "I'm good at guessing things like that. Like, I can sometimes tell who's at the door before it opens, or if anyone's been in my room, things like that."

Quoise stared intently at me. "Emma," she said. "I want you to close your eyes."

I did.

"Tell me what you see."

"Noth—" The word was half out of my mouth by habit before I realised it was a lie. "Trails," I said, standing taller. "Maybe. They're faint, sort of hovering in the air." I moved my head. "Oh, there are some on the ground, too."

"What do they look like?"

"Um..." I scrunched my eyes tighter, trying to figure out how to describe the strange sensation. I'd felt this before, I thought, though I couldn't place where.

Then it struck me. "Wait, Sanctuary is magical, right?"

"Yes, but—"

I waved a hand to silence her. Of course. Sanctuary was magical. I *had* felt this before—it was how I knew who was at the door or if someone had been in my room at home. It was just that with Sanctuary's magic, suddenly I could *see* these trails that previously I'd only ever *felt*.

"Ruby's," I began cautiously, "is kind of red, like her wings. Only... it smells like steel?" I ventured, not quite sure how to describe the cold, sharp smell. "Yours is bl—"

"No, no, stop, I don't want to know what mine looks like," Quoise said, and I opened my eyes to see her hands pressed over her ears.

"Did I do something wrong?" I asked, stomach dropping.

Quoise flung her arms wide and zoomed up into the air, looping-the-loop and beaming. "No! I can't believe I didn't notice it before!"

"Notice what?" I said, excited and confused.

"Emma," she said, grinning. "You're a Road Master!"

Instinctively I grinned back. "I have no idea what that means. But yay, right?"

Quoise laughed. "You can read the psychic footprints left behind by others. It's a rare talent, especially combined with the ability to Travel."

I blinked again. All those years of pretending I had special talents so I could stand out from my sparkly sister. Ha. Which reminded me... "Oh, it's Edge, by the way."

"Edge what?"

I grinned. "My name. Call me Edge, not Emma."

Quoise nodded. "Right you are, Road Master Edge." She nodded down at Veve, curled up asleep in the straw. "Well, Ye Of Many Talents, wake the guard-mutt and let's continue."

Grin plastered to my face, I nudged Veve with my foot and followed Quoise out of the stables. But Gem, stony-faced and arms crossed over her chest, stood firmly in Quoise's way. "You'll have to tell us sooner or later," she said.

Quoise stared at her. "I have absolutely no idea what you mean."

"Of course you do," Gem shot back. "But fine. We have to go anyway."

I blinked. "Already?"

"*Yes.*" Gem took my arm again and shepherded me away.

"Wait!" Quoise zoomed around in front of us. For a moment, I thought she might have decided to break down and tell Gemma whatever it was that was happening. But all she said was, "Do you want me to do the crossing for you?"

Gem, lips pursed, nodded curtly. "I have to be home at quarter past five."

Quoise smiled as though nothing had happened—like she hadn't been having secret conversations with another fairy about ominous shadows, and Gem hadn't tried to call her on it. "We'll have to hurry then. It's already quarter to."

Frowning, I glanced from one to the other. "I feel like I'm missing something here. Why does Quoise need to help us get back?" I might have misread the situation entirely, but I'd been under the pretty firm impression that I'd be able to cross back and forth to Sanctuary myself, at least at some stage.

"Sanctuary is a refuge," Quoise said, slipping into what I now knew was her lecture voice. "A refuge from all types of trouble, from all conflict. That includes time."

"You said that before. Wait." My eyebrows shot up. "Sanctuary has no time?"

Quoise nodded.

"So I could, like, stay here forever and no time would pass back home?"

Quoise laughed. "If only. No. Usually, the time skips happen completely at random. You might find you've returned right after you left, or hours later. But fairies can get you back at the right point in your personal timeline."

I ran my hand over one of the white-flowering bushes as we neared the garden alcove. "My personal timeline?"

"You've spent about half an Earth hour here. So we can get you back half an hour after you left. For anything else, you need a Time Master."

"Is that like a Road Master?" I stared at Gemma's back as she entered the alcove ahead of us, shoulders tense and hands fisted.

"I suppose so, in a way. Time Masters can control what time the travelling takes them to, so they can even go back before they left if they wanted to, and were strong enough. They're much more common than Road Masters. About one in six Travellers, actually. Here we are, then."

Before I had time to ask any more about Time Masters, Quoise had planted her seed and we stood back in the glade by the stream. Quoise said goodbye and disappeared.

I turned to Gem. "Okay, what's going on?"

She shook her head tightly, hands still curling and uncurling by her sides as we tromped through the bush toward the path. "I have to get home. It'll take too long to explain now. Look, get to school early tomorrow and I'll explain it first thing, okay?"

I nodded, bewildered. We reached the path and heading up to the stairs in the boulders.

"I have to go this way," Gem said, pointing further down the path. "I'll see you first thing." She gave me a quick hug and jogged away.

It wasn't until she'd rounded the corner out of sight that I realised I hadn't told her about my Road Mastery. "Never mind," I told Veve. "At least we had a good walk, right?"

Veve whuffed happily.

Some days, being a dog sounded really, really tempting.

7

FRIDAY MORNING SUCKED. Anna was allowed to drive us to school on Fridays, and I'd used everything I had to convince her to get in as early as possible (not easy, considering she hated mornings as much as I loved them).

I'd half expected Gemma to be waiting by the front gates for me, but she wasn't there, or by our lockers, or outside our roll call room—and she never arrived. Although I'd obviously been looking forward to discussing Sanctuary with her, it was having to sit by myself again that sucked most of all. I'd kind of gotten used to having a friend.

In science I slumped into a seat at the back, for once not feeling up to the scrutiny of the front row. And at least the seats on either side of me were taken, which meant the only spare seat for Scott— Mr King of Lateness—was down the front. Tragic.

Speak of the devil.

I rolled my eyes as he posed in the doorway and turned back to my desk, pointedly opening my textbook and reviewing the chapter we'd been set for homework. I could feel his disappointment radiating from here.

I allowed myself a smug smile—something I immediately regretted.

"Something funny?" he asked, crouching beside me. "'Cause I did the reading too, and I have to say, I didn't find it that amusing."

Frogging elephants, I could smell his deodorant. It wasn't *bad*, but I didn't want a reason to have to smell him *ever*, even if he smelled like rainbows.

He poked my shoulder. "Hey, I asked you a question. Or do you think you're so special you don't need to be polite?"

I exhaled and gave him my 'Are you serious?' look. Because, you know, he was *so* polite to me. "Scott, you wouldn't let the Queen ignore you."

"Oh, so you're even better than she is are you, Princess?"

I clenched my jaw and carefully turned a page in my textbook.

To my great relief, Scott stood. Sadly, the relief was short-lived: he tapped the girl next to me on the shoulder and gave her his 'charming' grin—I could see it blinding her out of the corner of my eye. "Can we switch seats?" he asked.

Confusion surfaced through her adoration. "Where's your seat?"

He shrugged, still beaming. "Any seat that isn't this one."

She stared at him, open mouthed, struggling to convince her brain to function in the face of his blinding magnificent.

I struggled to contain my snickering.

Scott leaned over her desk and lowered his voice. "I'd consider it a... special favour." He let the words hang, rich and full of promise.

I nearly choked. No thirteen-year-old should be able to use his voice like that. Life was so unfair.

The girl giggled, snatched up her things, and departed.

I bashed my forehead gently on my desk. When were these girls going to learn?

Up the front, Mrs Johnston tapped a marker on the desk. "If you're *quite* finished, Mr Harden." She raised an eyebrow and for a fleeting instant I thought maybe she knew what he was up to. Would she make him move for me?

No such luck. He slid into the now-empty seat beside me with polished grace and beamed back. "Sorry, Miss."

Frogging elephants, he practically glowed. And now he was glowing right next to me. I could have stabbed something.

Him, for preference.

The rest of the lesson proceeded with surprising and merciful monotony, and as Mrs Johnston signalled to us to pack up our things and head off to the final class of the day, I thought that maybe Scott's motivation for his little seat-switching act might have innocent after all. He *had* told me not to judge him.

I stacked my books and shoved my stationery back into my pencil case, eager for the day to be over so I could investigate Gem's mysterious absence.

As I zipped up my pencil case, I saw that my favourite pen was missing. I hunted around on the desk, even though my books sat neatly stacked and I could see plainly that it wasn't there. I checked the floor, the lab desk behind me... Nothing.

"Looking for something?"

I jumped. "What are you still doing here?" I snapped, preoccupied. It was only the first week of school, for crying out loud. I couldn't be losing stationery *already*.

Scott shrugged, shifting his books to one arm. "I thought I could help."

I glared at him. "Unless you can make pens appear out of thin air—no, wait," I said, tilting my head, "even if you can: *go away*." I resumed my search, scrabbling under the desks.

"Last chance, Emma," Scott said in an oddly calm tone of voice.

I snapped upright, bashing my head on the edge of a desk. "And what *precisely* is that supposed to mean?" I rubbed my head and stood, pain pulsing in time with my heartbeat.

"I lost my favourite pen. I told you I don't need your help, and now you're *threatening* me? What, because humiliating me in the corridors yesterday wasn't enough for you? Because you get off on making life miserable for me? Besides," I said, giving up on the pen and swiping my things off my desk. "It isn't here."

Scott's lips twitched as though he was struggling through some inner conflict. Like I cared. I hope he conflicted himself to death. "What if I could tell you where it is?"

I stopped dead. At first it wasn't so much the words as his tone, quiet and intense. And the look he was giving me was *weird*. I mean, hi, it was a pen. But then what he'd actually said hit me, and I narrowed my eyes. "You pig."

He blinked. "What?"

I strode toward him, furious. "Give it back."

He rocked away. "What?! No, I—"

"Give. It. Back!"

"I don't have! That's not what—"

Oh, that Mr Innocent act. "My *pen*," I yelled, dropping my books on the ground and launching myself at him. If he thought he could bully *me* and get away with it, he had another thing coming.

67

"Emma, calm down!" He stepped backwards, one hand up in surrender. "I don't have your pen! Honest!"

I punched him in the arm, not hard enough to really hurt him, but *boy* it felt good. "I've already lost my home, my friends, my *life*," I shouted. "And it was my *favourite pen*." I punctuated that last with solid pokes in the ribcage.

"Save me from the crazy-lady," he mock-yelled, fending me off with his free arm. "You're insane, Emma! I didn't take a thing."

I cried out in frustration and snatched his books from him, tossing them on the floor.

Scott scrabbled at them as they fell. "Hey, ow!" He jerked back, nursing his fingers. Blood seeped across them—a deep paper cut. "You *cut* me." He blinked in disbelief. "You actually cut me."

I stared in horror, heart hammering. "I didn't. You grabbed after your own books." But the anger was dying down, and guilt was more than happy to take its place. Despite my outburst, I hadn't meant to hurt him. I just wanted him to leave me alone.

Scott straightened coldly. "That was your last chance, Emma. I was going to tell you everything, and I could have told you where your stupid pen was. But you're a vicious, unstable, crazy-lady, and I'm so glad I found that out before it was too late."

He grabbed his books and stalked away. I stared, mouth open, my own books scattered on the floor like the aftermath of a very localised tornado. "Way to overreact," I muttered, but I wasn't sure if I meant him or me. Glumly, I began picking up my books.

At home that afternoon, I stripped off my uniform, pulled on some jeans, and hunted around for a clean shirt. As I did, a flash of orange under the bed caught my eye.

I stooped. My photo album.

I sank to the floor, cradling it in my lap. Grace, my best friend from Melbourne. I traced the cover picture with my fingers. We looked so happy. The picture had been taken after Year 7 camp last year. We'd had no idea that less than a year later we'd be torn apart; we'd planned to be friends forever.

The door opened and Mum stuck her head in. "Can you come help in the kitchen?"

I nodded, avoiding eye contact as tears breached my eyelashes.

"Are you okay?"

Sanctuary was wonderful, but... I shrugged, not knowing how to verbalise the ache inside me. "I miss home."

Mum came in and closed the door behind her. "I do too," she said as she knelt beside me.

I glanced up and my stomach dropped as I saw tears in her eyes too. I felt sick. "Why can't we just go home?" I asked, miserable. "They arrested someone. Doesn't that mean it's over?" I knew it wasn't that simple, but I had to ask, had to say it.

Mum smiled, but it was strained around the edges. "Even if they arrested the entire gang, your father doesn't have a job to go back to, Em. And I had to fight tooth and nail to get the position I'm in. If I told my bosses that I wanted to transfer back to Melbourne again..."

I nodded. "They wouldn't be happy." I knew it, but it didn't make things any better. "I miss home," I said again.

Mum scooped me into her arms. "You are home," she said. "You are home."

And as she rocked me like I was five years old again, patting my hair and humming, I could almost believe that I was.

8

I SAT AT the kitchen table on Sunday morning, contemplating a day's worth of homework, when the doorbell rang. Anna was shut in her room with music blaring and Mum and Dad were out in the yard, arguing over the awful prickly bushes around the side of the house, so I scraped my chair back with a tortured sound that pretty accurately described my feelings, and headed to the door.

My mood lifted considerably when I discovered Gem on the other side, beaming ear to ear.

"Hi," she said, a little breathless. That and her pinked cheeks suggested she'd walked over. She knew my house from riding the bus home with me, but all I knew was that she lived a little further down the line than I did. I'd have to get her address; if I'd had it, I'd have hunted her down yesterday to talk about Sanctuary.

"Sorry about Friday. I had to duck back into Sanctuary for something, and I messed up the timing getting back out. Mum nearly had a heart attack. She's a Time Master and she's been teaching me, but yeah. Anyway. Ready to go?"

I blinked, nonplussed by her casual dismissal of what sounded like a reasonably serious absence. "You... What?"

She grinned. "Oh, I kind of got stuck in transit or something. Mum went to Sanctuary to track me down, but I wasn't there, so she came back, but I wasn't here either, and I didn't get back to Earth until a couple of hours later. She was mental over it. It's never happened before. Crazy."

"Wait," I said. Somewhere in there the conversation had gotten away from me. "Your mum was in Sanctuary?"

"Oh, yeah, she's a Traveller too. Didn't Quoise tell you it can run in families? Mum's a Time Master, too, which is pretty handy, except when we cross paths, like Friday." She wrinkled her nose and screwed one eye shut. "But anyway!" Her blindingly bright smile returned. "Are you coming?"

"You know we have homework, right?" I raised an eyebrow at her. Wow. Family who were Travellers as well? Someone else's life had never sounded so appealing.

Her smile faded. "You're right. We could totally work on that right now. Or..." She grabbed my arm, utterly failing at keeping the excitement from her eyes. "We could go to Sanctuary and I could tell you what I know about what's going on."

It should have been a harder decision than it was, but really I only had a couple of maths problems to work through and a novel to start reading for English. It would take me a couple of hours, max. And after Gem's non-appearance on Friday, I was burning to know more about the shadows.

I slipped on some shoes, told Mum and Dad where I was going, and followed Gemma down to the glade. She headed off my questions, refusing to answer on the grounds that it would 'make more sense if I saw it', whatever 'it' was.

Once we'd crossed to Sanctuary, Gem led me up the hill to the stable.

One of the foals whinnied as we entered. "Poor baby," I crooned as I approached and hung my arm into the stall. "It's okay."

He snorted and flicked his tail before resting his chin back on the ground.

"Do you think their mother's disappearance has anything to do with the shadows?" I asked, sobering.

Gem nodded, also serious. "Absolutely I do. I've known Aphros—their mother—for years and there's no way she'd leave these little fellas alone for so long."

Finally, some answers. "So, any idea *how* her disappearance is related?"

"None at all."

"Do you know what the shadows are?"

"Nope."

"What's causing them?"

"No clue."

"So basically," I said, turning around and leaning my elbows on the door. "You have no idea what's going on."

Gem grinned. "Yup. Pretty much."

I rolled my eyes. "And that was so hard to tell me before."

Gem straightened, glancing furtively around. "Well, that's not all, of course. I'm not supposed to know this," she whispered. "But you know how Quoise and Ruby were talking about shadows in Sanctuary?"

I nodded.

"I know where they are. They're at the border crossing. That's what I wanted to show you."

She motioned me out of the stables and we headed farther up the hill. Close to the stables but hidden by a fringe of lacy-leafed trees, another larger building sat covered by rambling vines and fruit trees.

"The Lodge," Gem said with a wave. "It's pretty. We'll visit the main hall later. For now..." She gestured to a small doorway in what looked like the back of the building. We had to break a few vines to get the stiff door open. It creaked, protesting the whole way, but eventually I stuck my head in and saw a low hallway floored with some sort of glowing, polished material.

"Have you been here before?" I asked Gem as she shut the door behind us, only a little nervous.

"Not here-in-the-passageway here," Gem confessed as she squeezed past to lead the way. "This is an old emergency entrance. I only just discovered it. But I know where it leads, and I've been *there* loads of times."

I followed Gem down the passage for about twenty minutes until my skin began to crawl. I wasn't at all surprised when Gem halted.

In front of us stood another door, this one heavy looking and difficult to distinguish from the surrounding stone. "We have to be quiet," Gem breathed. "If the fairies see us..."

She trailed off, but I got the picture: this was one of those things that the fairies weren't keen on telling people. I wasn't sure how I felt about sneaking around and maybe—probably—breaking the rules, but before I could protest, Gem had eased the door open, checked for onlookers, and ushered me across this new hall and into another doorway. Light flashed as we passed through and I shivered. Then I saw the row of trees in front of us, and the shiver turned to a full-blown shudder.

"Well, this is the border," Gem said. "I'm sure you can see why."

I nodded. No wonder the fairies didn't want people here. Trees proceeded away from us in an orderly promenade before spreading out to form general bush some fifty paces away. But where the bush began, the scenery changed. On the near side, the trees stood tall and bore soft, delicate leaves. Lush grass carpeted the ground, and the scattered undergrowth was thick and healthy.

On the far side... Goosebumps prickled my arms. It *looked* like the kind of place the shadows would come from. The trees hunched and twisted, their leaves tinged in sickly yellow. The grass was mostly brown and crunchy, and the undergrowth, while definitely thick, was scrawny and full of thorns. To complete the picture, under every branch and bush and leaf, the shadows lurked, blacker than night.

"What is this place?" I asked.

"The Valley," Gem said softly. "It didn't always look so sick; it's gotten a lot worse in the last couple of months or so. Don't get too close," she added as I moved toward the promenade. "It's..." She rubbed her arms.

"Not right." I nodded. "I won't." I crouched a few paces away from Gem and stared. These shadows weren't as threatening as the ones that had bulged near the creek, but they still didn't feel right, and I studied them, trying to figure out why.

"The Valley," Gem said, sitting next to me. "It's... it's evil." Even though we sat cross-legged on the path almost as far from the border as we could get, she still shot it nervous glances, as though she expected it to come to life and pursue us.

"Yes," I said, impatient, because that much was blindingly obvious, "but what is it? Why is it there? Who lives there?"

Gem leaned back onto her hands and considered me. "You know about travelling, right? How it's powered?"

"A sacrifice of life," I said, nodding.

"Yes. Only it doesn't always have to be life."

I steeled myself against the images of stone altars and old, stained knives that flooded my mind. Still. Better than bloodied tiles. "The alternative isn't really an option, though, is it?"

Gem pursed her lips. "You'd think not."

My stomach twisted and I lowered my voice. "What, people do actually make death sacrifices to travel? But surely not of animals, or anything," I hurried on. "I mean, we use seeds. So they could use, I don't know, a plant or something, right?"

Gem met my gaze levelly. "Not seeds, Edge."

"And not plants?" I said, knowing the answer but not wanting to hear it.

"Not plants. The death of a plant is too cyclic. Its power is limited. You can travel using it, but not comfortably. I've heard... rumours, and they say it's like getting your brain squished out your nose. With a poker."

I winced. "Charming."

"Yeah, well, death magic is charming, what can I say." She shrugged. "And unlike life magic, it's a little hard to offer just a *bit* of death. Kind of an all-or-nothing type of magic."

I worked my tongue in my suddenly-dry mouth. "So... what do they use, then?"

"Animals, mostly. Small ones. Mice, rats, sometimes rabbits. Mostly."

I let the 'mostly' hang; some things I really didn't want to know. "So, fascinating though death magic is, didn't Quoise say you can't get to Sanctuary with it? What does this have to do with the border?"

Gem nodded. "You *can't* get to Sanctuary using death magic. That's why there's the border. That side isn't Sanctuary, Edge. It's the Valley of Death."

Ice trickled down my limbs. "You mean... the Valley is death?"

"Not literally," she added. "At least, I think not. I've never been there myself, seeing you have to use death magic to get there." She pulled a face.

"You can't just walk across?" I asked, surprised.

Gem shook her head. "Not without protection, or using death magic."

I rubbed away the goosebumps on my arms. "How is a place like that even allowed?" I muttered. "A whole place you have to murder to get to?"

Gem sighed and scratched at her wrist. "Well, I've heard the argument that death is a part of life. Mostly from people Mum suspected of *using* death magic, and as I like to remind them when I can, death isn't so much a *part* of life as the *end* of it, but hey." She grinned.

I rolled my eyes. "Lame, Gemma."

Her grin widened. "I know."

"So," I said, rolling a blade of grass between my fingers. "Do you think that's why it exists? Because death does?"

Gem shook her head. "I… I heard a rumour once that it used to be a part of Sanctuary. Mum says she's never heard that though, and of course the fairies won't talk about it. I'm not sure if they don't know or if they're hiding something, but anyway."

"What about death magic?"

"As far as I know, that's always been around. It's nasty stuff, though," she said in hushed tones. "I've heard it contaminates you forever, corrupting you and making you evil, and if it goes too far you can't get into Sanctuary anymore."

"So what's across the border, then?" I asked, tossing the grass away.

"Nothing."

"Yeah, all those trees and mountains sure look like nothing to me." I raised a sceptical eyebrow.

"Well *I* don't know, do I? Do I look like the kind of person who murders small animals for fun?"

I raised the other eyebrow. "What about all those people that travel using death magic? No one's ever reported what's over there?"

Gem folded her arms. "Look, I don't know, okay? Stop harping on about it. It's the Valley, home to death and murder and everything nice and wonderful like that. I don't see why you're so obsessed with it."

"I'm not obsessed, I'm trying to figure out what's going on," I said, leaning over my knees.

We fell silent, me staring at the border and Gemma aimlessly plucking grass.

If you only glanced across the border, the trees didn't look much different from some I'd seen up in the Snowy Mountains, stunted and twisted from wind and snow. But even without using my Road Mastery, a longer look was enough to show that something about the Valley's trees was off. The twist of limb suggested torture, the yellow of the leaves illness and decay. It was impossible to forget, once you knew, that you were looking at the land of death.

I shivered and looked back at Gem. "I thought you said nothing could live there."

She glanced toward the Valley. "Nothing does. The fairies say the trees aren't really alive; they're just pretending to be, like a mask on a corpse."

"Lovely." I scrunched up my nose.

"Their comparison, not mine." Gem shrugged.

I hugged my knees to my chest. "And the shadows are concentrated here?"

"I think so. I mean, the fairies won't say anything, but I've poked around all over, and these are the thickest I've found anywhere. Why? Did you think of something?"

"Not yet." I shook my head. "Just... thinking."

"Sure. Think away."

I tilted my head. I was missing something here. Something right in front of me was a big clue, I knew it, but I couldn't figure out what.

Sighing, I rested my head on my knees and closed my eyes. We shouldn't be here, and no doubt the fairies had their reasons. If they hadn't told us about this place, probably there was nothing we could do anyway.

Images of bloodstained tiles flashed past my thoughts again, but I shoved them away, concentrating instead on a dim smudge in the dark that I couldn't quite catch—Gemma's presence—and... I bolted upright, eyes still closed.

"What, what it is?" Gem asked, scrambling to her feet beside me.

"Shh." It was hard to tell, but in places the darkness behind my closed eyelids seemed blacker than the rest. I opened my eyes. Right where the shadows were.

"They're darker," I muttered. I stared at them, teased by the knowledge that they were different from regular shadows but unable to figure out why. My gaze roved over them, back and forth, and then—ah ha. "Gemma, look at the shadows."

"I *have* been."

I shook my head. "Look closer. They're going the wrong way."

She stiffened next to me. "Oh my gosh, they are too!" She glanced up at the dusky sky above us. "Not that there's a sun here anyway. Which,"—she frowned—"the light issue here has always puzzled me. How are there shadows in the first place? How is there light?"

I glanced around. "That's another point. Those shadows are more like normal Earth shadows." Everywhere else the shadows were soft and indistinct, blurry and gentle. "So something in the Valley has to be causing them?" I asked, calculating the angles of the shadows again. It definitely looked like the light source was behind them, somewhere out there in front of us in the Valley.

"Looks like." Gem rubbed her arms again, probably to shift goosebumps like I had on my arms. "I knew they were no good," she muttered.

A flash of gold and pale green caught my eye through the trees. "What was that?" I pointed.

Gem jumped. "What?" She stared into the trees, breath held and ready to flee.

"I saw something," I said, lowering my arm. "I promise. A flash of light maybe, or something pale."

Gem shook her head and backed away. "Nothing lives in the Valley."

"How do you know?" I said, peering into the trees, hoping to catch another glimpse.

"Because I've been here forever and I know what I'm talking about, and no one lives there, okay?"

I glanced back at her. "Wow, okay then. Maybe it was a trick of the light, or something." It hadn't been and I knew it. I got up and moved closer to the border, heart hammering. *I shouldn't be here. I shouldn't be here!* But the mystery of the shadows and now the flash bound me fast.

"Emma, can we just go now please?" Gem said, shifting. "You've seen everything, you know everything I know. Let's go. This place is creepy."

"Exactly," I said, still staring into the trees. "But the shadows are clearly coming from here, so it's worth investigating, right?" And whatever it was that had flashed was somehow related. I stepped closer again. This was Sanctuary. Really serious bad stuff didn't happen here. If it had been that dangerous, surely the fairies would have blocked off the path. Well, with more than a couple of unlocked doors, anyway, I added guiltily.

"Emma, there's nothing over there. We need to go." Gem's voice had risen several tones and when I glanced back at her, she just about jittered.

My lips quirked; usually she couldn't *wait* to bend the rules to suit herself, and I...

I stared back at the awful trees and swallowed. I wouldn't be caught dead doing something this stupid. I sighed. Gemma was right. Time to go.

I turned, and another flash caught the corner of my eye. I whirled back to face it. "There!" I said, pointing. "I saw it again, right there!"

"It was probably just light on a leaf," Gemma snapped. "I'm going."

I regarded her carefully. "Do those look like the kind of leaves that reflect light?"

She glared at them out of the corner of her eye, unwilling to let her gaze linger on the place. "Maybe. It's the Valley. It doesn't operate by normal rules. Who knows what it might do?"

I peered through the trees. Was that a clearing in there? Maybe a clearing. I moved left, trying to see around a particularly large, scrubby bush.

"Edge, you're making me nervous. I'm serious."

Blah, moving left just meant a fallen tree was in the way instead. I stepped closer to the border, almost toe-to-toe with it.

"Edge, come back here, right now!"

I looked back at Gem—and as I did, gold and pale green flashed a third time in the corner of my eye. I whipped around.

I overbalanced. My foot came down on the border—and something wrapped around my ankle and jerked me into the Valley.

9

GEM SCREAMED.

I may have squeaked a little bit.

Okay, I may have squeaked a lot.

"Edge! Edge, come back!" Gem shrieked.

Sounded like a fantastic idea to me—but how? The grip around my ankle had tightened, dragging me deeper and deeper into the land of death.

My feet skimmed the ground, trees blurring past, and I only just had time to note that I'd been right about the clearing before I was dragged through it and back into the trees. Frogging elephants, this was *exactly* what that happened when you broke the rules! I should never have let Gem drag me to the border like that in the first place. Argh!

Gradually the pace slowed—though my pulse didn't—and I could see the trees more clearly. Their twisted trunks had split in places, revealing oozing red sap that looked scarily like old, bubbled blood. I swallowed hard and wished I could speed up again.

Just don't look. I told myself. I closed my eyes, but motion sickness threatened to empty my stomach, so instead I stared upwards, concentrating on the glimpses of sky and trying to watch where I was being taken so I'd know the way back.

Ahead, the ground sloped upwards, and through a sudden gap in the trees I saw a mountain rising to each side. I was headed straight for the pass in between. The Valley proper.

I squeaked and struggled against the force around my ankle. "Let me go!" I clawed at it, but there was nothing to grab, nothing to struggle *against* except constant, inexorable pressure.

My heart hammered in my ears. "Let me go!"

The force swerved me to the left; I headed now toward the mountain instead of the pass. I wasn't sure if that was better or worse—and before I could decide, the force around my ankle disappeared.

I stopped dead and stumbled to the ground. Clutching my ribs, I gasped, trying to work the air back into my lungs. It tasted fetid and ripe, and I choked, tears springing up.

My coughing sounded out of place in the oppressive silence and I stopped abruptly. The only sound was blood rushing past my eardrums.

"Where are you?" I spun in a slow circle, trying to find my captor. "Show yourself!"

Nothing appeared.

Shadows lurked under the trees and my breath hitched in my throat. "Show yourself!"

The hair on the back of my neck prickled and I whirled around, sure that someone was watching me. But there was nothing there except the awful trees with their oozing bark and strange, yellowed leaves that didn't move.

A sharp crack rang out and I squeaked. I whirled right around again before realising it was the sound of a dead branch falling. I gasped, pulse trilling and adrenalin lifting me up on my toes.

The trees loomed and the thick air pressed down, stifling. It was hot here, much hotter than in Sanctuary—and brighter. The sky was the blue-green of dusk, rather than Sanctuary's pearly grey dawn, though there was still no sun to be seen.

I shivered. Time to get out of here. I turned again, looking for something to orient myself. I recognised a fallen log and stepped toward it.

The invisible force clamped down on my ankle, rooting me to the spot. I clawed at my ankle, but there was nothing to see, nothing to grab. I panted, fighting panic. What *was* this thing?

And then I felt it: the slightest breath of wind in a heavy, dead land—and I couldn't tell if I sensed it physically or with my Road Mastery.

I stared at the edges of the clearing and there, toward the mountain—the flash of gold.

Help me. The words weren't spoken but I heard them clearly nonetheless, a soft suggestion like the faintest bells on a clear, crisp morning, or silver glimmering through fog.

I stilled, heart pounding, but for the moment in control of the panic. "Who are you?"

Please, the voice begged. *You must set me free.*

"Who are you?" I repeated, palms growing sweaty. "*Where* are you?"

Help.

I threw my hands up. "I can't help you if I don't know who you are!" Especially in the Valley, where the only residents were those who'd used death magic to get here. Those kind of people I didn't *want* to help. I struggled, pulling on my leg, but the grip tightened.

You can help me.

"How?"

Please. Your Road Mastery. Please! Desperation filled the speaker's voice and their grip on my ankle tightened.

I was losing feeling in my toes. What could I do? I couldn't just agree to help someone when I didn't know who they were or what they were asking—especially in the Valley.

A gasp echoed in my mind, accompanied by a breath of not-wind that felt green and gold, and smelled clean, like mint. Mint wasn't a death smell; it was too fresh, too green and alive.

I seriously couldn't feel my toes, and the gasps had turns to sobs, coming in raggedy breaths. I had no doubt that the being, whoever it was, could keep me here until my foot dropped off, or I agreed—or they died, I added as a scream, shrill and hoarse, cut across the sobs.

I took a deep breath and hoped that this wasn't about to be the last stupid thing I ever did. "Okay," I said. "Okay. I'll help you. What do I do?"

Your Road Mastery. Help me, please!

I closed my eyes and searched. There, toward the centre of the Valley—green and gold light flashed and pulsed in time with the screams in my head. I reached out toward it, and it grabbed at me like a drowning person. "Stay still!" I shouted as it choked me. "I'm trying to help! Just stay still!"

The flailing paused for an instant and in the calm I sensed something else: a deep darkness behind the green, building like a storm cloud. I snatched at the green-and-gold and pulled, gasping for air even though I wasn't actually moving. The green tore away from the black, and the sense of connection I had with it snapped.

The pressure on my ankle disappeared, and my Road Mastery blacked out. I gasped as the blood flowed back into my numb foot and my toes tingled with pins and needles.

"Hello?" I called, shaking my foot. "Hello, where are you?" I had no idea who I'd just helped, but if it got them away from the blackness, that had to be good, right? Shudders ran up and down my body. "Are you okay?" I shouted. "Please be okay..."

The mint-fresh breeze swept over me. *Flee.*

The urgency in the voice hammered my senses and terror froze me, mouth open wide.

It will sense you. Flee!

My heart pounded so hard I clutched my chest to hold it in. I backed away, staring wide-eyed at nothing, and licked at my lips.

Run! the voice said faintly, just on the edge of hearing.

I turned and ran.

My heart pounded as I dodged branches and jumped logs, running faster than I'd ever run in my life. The air suffocated me and my lungs burned with the effort of breathing.

Adrenaline shot through my chest; something had grabbed at my shoulder. I whirled around, nearly tripping, but all I could see was the trees. I bit back panic and ran again.

Something grabbed my other shoulder, tangling in my shirt. I didn't have breath left to scream. I reached up to swat it away—and my fingers met rough bark.

For one long moment I froze, eyes wide as I stared at the tree looming over me. Its twig-fingers snatched at my shirt. I shrieked, batting at it while my skin crawled all over.

I wrenched free and ran.

The trees grabbed at me. *"Come to us,"* their leaves shushed in the still, heavy air. *"Come, let us hold you, let us touch you. Give us your light, your soul, so sweet, so sweet your blood."*

Tears streamed down my cheeks. Wet strands of hair tangled over my face, blinding me, choking me. My lungs burned. I gasped. I sobbed. Fear caught in my throat as I pushed through branches that whispered of devoured souls and death. Something caught my ankle. I stumbled, fell.

My fingers grazed the ground as I caught my balance. A shadow leapt up, tangling itself around my wrist. It dragged me down and smothered me in a cold so heavy it could only be death. *"So sweet, so sweet your soul. Let me live."*

I screamed, flailing. "Let me go! Let me go!"

Darkness closed out my vision, shadows multiplying faster than rats as they surged over me.

"Help!" I screamed as I lashed out at shadows and found nothing to hit. "Somebody, help!"

The shadows flattened me on the ground. My heart thundered in my ears. I fought for breath, trying to surface through their icy weight. What had I done to deserve this? I'd helped! I'd *helped*!

Dread flooded over me as I realised that that was exactly what I'd done. How could I have been so stupid? Everyone *knew* you didn't help random magical strangers!

The weight of my stupidity settled like a knot in my stomach, burning copper and hot. The shadows sprawled over me completely, but through the fire of anger and shame in my belly I could feel the dirt beneath my fingers, under my chest and against my knees. I would *not* die because of stupidity. That was the kind of thing Anna would do.

I forced myself to quit struggling, letting the avalanche of shadows pin me. I concentrated on breathing. The shadows pressed down too hard for me to fill my lungs deeply, but at least I could stop hyperventilating. I would not die here like this. I would *not*.

"Hold you, touch you... So warm and light, alive, we want your life."

You can't have it. "Three. Two. One." I heaved up off the ground, exploding forward like a runner out of the blocks. I had one chance to escape. The shadows wouldn't let me slip away again.

"Come back, come home to us." Pain seared my calves as branches raked them, but I clenched my jaw and ran. I felt the shadows snap behind me, leaving icy burns in their wake. Leaves fell like acid rain, stinging my skin, smoking my clothes. Sweat clouded my eyes, and fire raged in my throat.

I wouldn't make it. I didn't have anything left to keep going.

A beam of light shot through the trees and I pushed toward it. Green, and the smell of mint. Through streaming eyes I saw more green, proper green, the green of healthy leaves and grass. The border. *Sanctuary*.

I shrieked for all I was worth and lunged, one last, giant surge of effort to get me across the line. Branches grabbed my hair. I jerked my head away, screaming as my hair tore. I stumbled, fell—and the world slowed, brightened, and I reached out to steady myself against a tree, a tree with smooth, unsplit bark and healthy leaves. I stared at my hand on the trunk and the world stilled.

My chest heaved. My whole body was alight, but I was touching a tree, and it wasn't trying to devour me. I sobbed, crumbling to the ground. I'd made it.

And then Gem was there, shouting and kneeling beside me, cradling me in her lap. Bright gems flashed around her head, and I convulsed with laughter that hurt like a mule kick, because Gem and her gems. The gem-like fairies fluttered against me and soothed away some of the pain, and darkness edged my vision again—only this time it was a quiet dark, soft and warm and gentle, and I was so happy to surrender.

The last thing I heard was Gem: "I'd better get her home."

10

I CAME TO as Gem dragged me to my feet in the clearing by the stream, and blinked blearily at the long shadows that stretched across the ground. They filtered through the fog in my head and I jolted upright, screaming.

"Hey! Hey, it's okay," Gem soothed, holding me tight. "We're home. It's okay."

I collapsed against her and sobbed. My muscles ached and my skin stung where the burning leaves had fallen and the trees had scratched.

"Shh, it's okay." Gem stroked my hair. "What happened? What was it?"

I shook my head, burying my face against her shoulder. How could I possibly explain? Shudders wracked my body as I remembered the trees, their twig-fingers snatching and grabbing, their whispers of death and destruction. I sobbed harder.

"It's okay," she said. "You don't have to tell me. It's okay."

I hugged her back as the sobs gradually ebbed, relieved beyond words that she wasn't going to make me talk about it. Images raced across my mind, black shadows, grabbing trees, blood on white tiles, staring eyes, twigs snatching and snapping...

"Let's get you home." Gem pushed me back to arm's length. "Yes?"

I nodded and took in a deep, shuddery breath, forcing the flow of images away, washing them down a mental drain. "Yes."

She wrapped her arm around my waist, and guided me toward the path. I tried to keep my gaze from wandering, tried not to see the shadows that dappled the clearing, but they drew my eye like corpses. As we reached the beginning of the path, my gaze strayed across the creek. I gasped and whipped my eyes shut, stumbling against Gemma. The shadows there were the same as the ones from the Valley.

"Come hooome..."

By the time we reached the main track, the sun had disappeared behind mounting thunderheads.

Gem glanced at the sky, biting her lip, and herded me along faster. I couldn't bring myself to care about something as mundane as a storm. The shadows, the same ones that had just tried to kill me, were here, in the real world, by the creek. Once I got home, I was never going outside again.

The rain broke as we headed toward my back gate and it was almost a relief. It took the pressure out of the air and seemed to melt the darkness away; as Gem eased me into the yard I saw that the shadows near the prickly bushes had shrunk.

Veve whuffed, curled tight and warm in her kennel, tail thump-thumping against it. Gem ignored her and steered me to the back door, where she stopped and removed our shoes. She eased me into the laundry, rummaged around for something to get the worst of the rain off, then stuck her head out into the hall.

"Gemma?" Anna joined us in the laundry. I had no doubt that I looked a complete mess, but my stomach was rolling and my vision blurring too much for me to care, and I just wanted to crawl into bed and die.

"What happened?"

"She fell," Gemma said, staring evenly at Anna.

Anna stared back, eyebrow raised—but then she sighed and opened the door to the hall. "Mum and Dad have gone down to the shops. You need a hot shower and bed."

I nodded. That sounded heavenly.

"I'll take her from here," Anna said curtly, glancing at Gemma.

My chest tightened. *No*, I wanted to say. *Don't be angry at Gemma. She saved me. She tried to stop it. It isn't her fault. She brought me home.* But all I could do was follow as Anna swept me into the hallway, sending one last grateful glance to Gemma over my shoulder.

Gemma nodded and let herself out.

"Come on," Anna said. "Let's get you warm."

Covered in scrapes and bruises and aching from head to toe, it didn't take too much effort to convince Mum that school on Monday was a bad idea, though thankfully I'd been able to convince her I'd only fallen down the stairs by the creek and didn't need to see a doctor.

And when nightmares kept me from sleeping again on Monday night and I woke on Tuesday pale and shaky, Mum herself suggested that I spend another day in bed. If it meant avoiding Gemma's questions and the outdoors for another day, I was all over it.

The rain continued through to Tuesday afternoon, cascading over the house and washing away the heat and dust. When it finally stopped, the world seemed bright and clean—shadow-free.

So Wednesday morning I rose and dressed for school—stiffly—and by the time I climbed on board the bus, the whole incident in the Valley could have been only another one of the bad dreams it had inspired.

A freaky, horribly realistic dream that left me spooking at shadows and avoiding close proximity with trees, but a dream nonetheless. *See me convince myself*, I thought wryly.

The only thing I couldn't dismiss, the part that seemed to grow more and more real instead of fading, was the voice. Even now I could close my eyes and tune out the noises of the bus, hearing the soft, urgent call. The stink of oil and petrol, musty seats and sweat-stained children could easily fade to mint with a streak of gold, and the waft of air caused by the passing of other passengers could be the breeze of the voice on my cheek.

The bus grumbled to a halt outside the school. I waited for the first rush to disembark before slinging my bag over my shoulder and following. As I jumped down the final step, I jammed my hat firmly on my head so I wouldn't get into trouble for arriving in 'inappropriate uniform'. The hat wouldn't stay on with my hair in a ponytail, so I marched onto the grounds with the brim pulled low and my chin up in the air so I could see, refusing to acknowledge the fact that this particular hat style also shut down my peripheral vision and helped me ignore the trees.

I jumped when a leaf skittered across my path.

I headed toward my locker, and with my hat down and chin up I nearly didn't see Scott lurking in a corner. I wondered if I could pretend I hadn't, but it was too late: he'd seen me and was heading over. Sigh.

"Feeling high and mighty this morning, Princess?" he sneered.

A certain coldness in his voice brought back memories of the shadows. "Thank you, Scott," I said brightly. "I had a lovely long weekend. I had over a hundred Scott-free hours. Too bad you can't have any."

I cringed internally. Maybe that was a little harsh. *Not* that I was going to take it back. I plastered on the fakest smile I could manage, and pushed past him to get to my locker.

He moved his shoulder to block me. "Oh, we're in a hurry are we, Princess?"

I tried to move him and my heart fluttered in momentary panic as I realised how strong he was. "Yes." I kept my voice level. "Considering the *bell* is about to go."

Scott lounged back against my locker. "True. But since I'm here, and your *Scott-free* hours seem to have ended, I have something to tell you."

"I don't want to hear it." I removed my hat and crammed it into my school bag. "I want to get to my locker. Move. Please." I glared at him.

"Or what, Princess?" Scott donned a lazy smile that said he had all the time in the world. "Besides, don't you want to hear my news?"

"Tsh." I threw my hands up in the air, frustration and anger burning away my fear. "Was Friday not clear enough for you, Scott? *I don't like you.* I will *never* like you, so please do us all a favour and *quit trying.*" I swung my bag at him, gently enough not to damage my lunch but firmly enough that he knew I was serious.

"Edge!"

I glanced down the hall to see Gem striding toward us, brow wrinkled in concern. "What's going on here?" she asked as she arrived and stood with hands on hips.

"*Scott* is going on here," I said, rolling my eyes. "I can't get to my locker." The first bell rang. "And now we're late."

Gem turned to Scott. "You leave Edge alone," she said sternly, and I felt a rush of warmth.

Scott snickered. "Edge? Do you call her that because no one wants her, so she has to hang out on the *edge*?"

Gem widened her eyes. "Wow, Scott! Did you think of that all by yourself? Oh my gosh, you're *so* clever." She fluttered her eyelashes at him and I snickered behind my hand. "Besides," she said, shrugging. "Last I heard, *some people* were pretty keen on our Emma here." She slung an arm casually around my shoulders and raised her eyebrow pointedly at Scott.

The outrage on his face was priceless. I wriggled my fingers at him, grinning.

But Gem wasn't finished. "So," she said. "Why don't you just move out of the way and let *Edge* into her locker? We're late."

"Oh yeah?" He squared his shoulders, posturing. A moment ago it might have been intimidating, but with Gem by my side I felt stronger, more sure of myself. "What are you going to do?" Scott continued. *"Tell a teacher?"*

"Tell a teacher what?"

All three of us jumped as Mrs Johnston appeared.

"Um, nothing," Scott said hastily, cheeks colouring as he edged away from my locker.

Gem shoved me at my locker, muttering, "Get your stuff." She turned to Mrs Johnston, eyes wide in practiced innocence. "I was going to *tell* you, Mrs Johnston," she said, "that Scott here wouldn't let Emma into her locker, and now"—the second bell punctuated her sentence perfectly—"we're late."

Mrs Johnston peered at Scott. "Is this true?"

His blush deepened. "Er, no, Miss. I was, um, offering to help Emma with her books."

I snickered behind the locker door as I shoved my bag in and grabbed my books out. Slamming the door shut, I turned just in time to see Mrs Johnston give him the Look.

"Get. To class."

He stared at the floor. "Yes, Miss. I don't..." He gazed up at her through his lashes. "I mean, can I have a late slip?"

"*No*, Scott. Class. *Now*."

He disappeared down the hallway.

"Thanks, Mrs Johnston," I said, avoiding eye contact.

"Miss Caro," she said, ignoring me. "Are you wearing makeup?" She arched an eyebrow and I snuck a glance at Gem.

Again, with the practiced, wide-eyed innocence. "No, Mrs Johnston," Gem said, shaking her head and looking horrified. "Why would I do something like that? I'm a your star student!" Her eye contact didn't waver. I restrained my own eyes from rolling.

"Hmm." Mrs Johnston scrutinised her face once more, then nodded. "Here." She drew two late passes out from her pocket and scrawled her signature on them. "Get to class."

We snatched up the passes and scattered like mice. I shot Gem a look as we hurried down the hall. "You are so wearing makeup," I murmured.

She shrugged, and the movement drew my attention to her fingers, clutching her books.

"You're wearing *nail polish* too?"

"It's pale pink!" she protested as she slowed outside our roll call room. "You can barely see it!"

"I think," I muttered as we slipped into the classroom, "we need to talk."

She snorted. "We do. But not about that. About the Valley."

My stomach dropped as we handed our passes to the teacher and took the only remaining seats, one on each side of the room.

Oh yes. We needed to talk.

11

MY ART CLASS was kept in over recess because one of the boys decided to be a moron and fling paint around the room, so I didn't get a chance to talk with Gemma until lunchtime. By then, I'd had all morning to remember that my nightmares were actually well founded, and I really didn't *want* to talk. I couldn't go home to Melbourne because it still wasn't safe, and I didn't want to go to Sanctuary because *it* might not be safe, so I might as well start facing the fact that I was stuck here in Nowra, nowhere to go except home and school.

Gem plonked herself on the bitumen opposite me and raised expectant eyebrows. "Well?"

"Well what?" I said, unwrapping my sandwich with complete and absolute focus.

"Well *what happened*?" She leaned toward me, eyes alight.

"I don't want to talk about it." I took a bite of my PBJ sandwich.

"Edge!" She flung her hands in the air, sandwich lettuce flying. "You can't go around having death-defying adventures and doing things that aren't even supposed to be *possible*, and then not *tell* me about them!"

"Watch me," I muttered. Diversion time. "So what's with the makeup?"

"Oh, I've been wearing it forever," she said breezily, unwrapping her own lunch. "You just haven't noticed."

I snorted. "Yeah, because we all know how unobservant I am."

She grinned and took a bite out of her salad roll.

"And the nail polish? I know for sure you haven't been wearing *that* 'for ages'."

Gem shrugged. "A present from my cousin on the weekend. I had to try it out." She wriggled the fingers on her left hand at me. "It's subtle. No one will even notice."

"Except me."

"Right, except you, but you're my bestie. You're supposed to notice stuff like that." She took another bite of sandwich, chewed thoughtfully, and swallowed. "So, is the whole Valley episode the reason we're eating in the middle of the overtly treeless car park today?"

I stuck out my tongue. "It's warm here."

"Unlike the freezing twenty-seven C it is every-where else, you mean."

I stared at her, stomach churning. "Are you really going to make me talk about it?"

"Yup." She beamed at me.

I shook my head. "Don't look like that. It's not... I mean..." I sighed. "It wasn't exciting, okay?"

Her face grew serious, and I felt the words well up. I wasn't ready to confess my family's past to her, but this bit, this slice... She deserved that much. "I haven't slept properly since Sunday. I'm twitching at shadows, I can't go near trees without flinching, and the wind rustling through leaves sends nerves through my stomach every time. I'm jumpier than a grasshopper on crack and I'm sick of it." I pressed my face into my knees. "And I think I did something really stupid." I'd almost managed to forget that bit.

I felt Gem's hand on my shoulder. "Hey, it's okay, Edge. I'm sorry. I didn't realise."

I nodded without lifting my head off my legs. "I know. It's fine."

"So..." Gem hesitated. "What's this stupid thing you did?"

I sighed. If I was never going back to Sanctuary again, I should at least give her a reason. "So you know how in, like, every story in existence, you're warned not to agree to help someone magical when you don't know who they are?"

Gem nodded.

"Especially in somewhere like the Valley, right?"

"Edge," she said carefully. "What are you saying?"

"There was a voice," I said picking at my lunch. "It was the one who dragged me in there. I told you I'd seen a flash of gold," I said, raising my eyes to meet Gem's. "It... it asked for my help. Asked me to come to it." I stared at my sandwich again, fiddling with the crust. "I said I would, because it had me by the ankle, and my foot was going numb."

Did I dare tell her about ripping the green trace from the shadows? My pulse skipped. "But then I agreed, and it disappeared, and told me to flee." I looked up at Gem again, anchoring myself, fighting back the panic. "So I did." I held up my arms, still covered in scabbed scratches. "The trees fought back. The shadows nearly got me."

Tears prickled my eyes as Gem reached over and squeezed my hand. "Edge, that's awful. I'm so sorry."

I shrugged, sucking in air and forcing the memories away. "I'll live."

She shook her head. "I don't know, though. I don't think the voice can have been that bad, can it? I mean, it told you to run."

I shrugged. "It was scared of the shadows too, I think." Echoes of the green voice's fear skittered down my spine.

"Well, there you go, then." Gem shrugged. "I think it'll be all right."

The back of my neck prickled. "Let's go," I muttered, gathering my things. "Scott's listening."

Gem's eyes widened. "I was about to say that. How did you know?"

"He's standing right behind me." *Duh.* I wrinkled my brow.

"I know," Gem said. "I see him. But he's *behind* you. How did you know it was him?"

My stomach flipped as I realised I'd been using my Road Mastery. I sighed again and stood with my lunch in hand. "Come on," I said. "I'll tell you on the way."

We headed past the playground and through the walkway that led to the main lawn.

"I'm a Road Master," I said without preamble as we found an empty patch of grass.

Gem stopped short. "You're kidding."

I shrugged and flopped down. I crammed the last of my sandwich into my mouth in an effort to still the nerves. If Gem laughed at me, I might just die on the spot.

Gem shook her head and plonked down beside me, face splitting into a beaming grin. "Edge! Why didn't you *tell* me! That is *so cool!*" She crushed me with a hug. "You're awesome!"

I swallowed and grinned back. "Thanks." At least that was one good thing I wouldn't have to give up.

"So." Gem guzzled down the last of her own sandwich. "Tell me, oh great and mighty one. How good are you?"

I laughed, pleased by the distraction. "Gem, I only found out less than a week ago. I haven't exactly had much chance to practice."

She rolled her eyes at me. "You might not have had much practice, but I'll bet you can still tell how good you are. Go on." She motioned with the last half of her sandwich. "Close your eyes and tell me who's behind you."

"Don't be ridiculous," I said.

Gem's lips twitched. "Just do it."

I closed my eyes. "We're not in Sanctuary, Gemma. I'm telling you, this is point—"

I gasped. They were faint, the visual equivalent of a slightly off-station radio, but all around me colours wove and tangled—and the harder I concentrated, the more focused they became, until I could see clearly the traces of people sitting within about ten meters of me, and could sense with varying degrees of clarity people all the way back to the playground.

I'd sensed people before of course, but that had been faint, or people I knew. But now that I knew what I was looking for—now I'd been exposed to Sanctuary's magic a few times—my brain seemed to have grasped the idea with enthusiasm.

"Oh. My. Gosh!" I said, grinning. "I rock!"

Gem exploded in laughter, throwing her head back and flapping her hands in delight. "Yes, dear Edgey, you do." She flopped sideways with her head resting on my leg and sighed happily. "So *that's* how you could tell where the shadows were coming from."

I nodded.

"Now we'll be able to get to the bottom of them for sure!"

I tensed, and the memories crowded back in. "Maybe," I murmured noncommittally. I'd told Gem enough for one day. I couldn't bear telling her that I wasn't going back to Sanctuary as well.

"I'm still worried about Aphros being missing," Gem said as we headed down the locker corridor after school.

I nodded as my stomach knotted. I'd forgotten about the motherless unicorn twins. "Yeah. I'll bet anything it's related to the stupid shadows."

Gem nodded back. "Absolutely. Hang on," she said as we neared the bathrooms. "Two seconds." She dumped her bag at my feet and disappeared.

I leaned against the wall and closed my eyes, glad hump day was over for another week.

"There you are, Princess."

I groaned. Why did the world hate me so much?

"Aww, Princess. Still too high and mighty to talk to me?"

I heaved a sigh and dragged my eyes open. "What do you want, Scott?"

"I just wanted to tell you that your little *friend"*— he pulled a face—"is safe with me."

I blinked. "Am I supposed to have *any* clue what you're talking about?"

Predictably, he ignored me. "Oh, and here." He thrust something green at me and I reached out reflexively. He stalked away.

I looked down. My pen.

Gem reappeared. "What's up?" she said. "You look like a stunned mullet."

I searched for something coherent to say, failed spectacularly, and held up my pen. "What world are we in?"

Gem grabbed up her bag and took me by the hand, patting it comfortingly as she led me down the hallway. "Now, I want you to concentrate, Emma. This is very serious. We are on this lovely little planet called *Earth*," she soothed. "It has trees that stay where they're planted and shadows that don't try to eat you, and this weird little species called humans who are supposed to be really smart but, if you ask me, are actually spectacularly dumb."

I laughed and shook her away, wriggling the pen at her. "My pen. Scott had it all along."

Gem shook her head. "Little wretch. We ought to feed him to the shadows."

I flinched to a halt. "No one deserves the shadows."

Meekly, Gem took my arm again. "I'm sorry, Edgey. You're right of course."

I nodded, and headed out toward the bus stop.

"We'll figure this out," Gem continued. "In fact, why not figure it out tonight?" She pulled out her phone, dialled, and held it to her ear.

I waited patiently to see what she had in mind.

"Mum? Hi, yeah, good. Look, can I stay at Edge's tonight? Yes? Awesome! Thanks! Bye!" She hung up and raised an eyebrow at me. "Think your parents will go for it? Your house is closer to the creek is all, otherwise I'd invite you to mine."

Nerves tingled through me. It didn't matter what Gem said, I was not going near that place ever again. But a sleepover might be fun—and it might keep the nightmares at bay. I shrugged. "Let's see."

A few minutes later, everything was settled: Gem would come and stay the night, ostensibly to help me catch up on the work I'd missed, and with any luck the company would calm me enough so I could actually sleep.

We approached the bus stop and a shadow flicked over me. I jumped.

"Hey, it's okay," Gem said. "It was only a bird. The shadows can't get you here."

I stopped again, searching out her eyes. I had to tell her that I wasn't going back. "What about in Sanctuary, though?"

She held my arms from behind, steering me into line. "Hey, that was the Valley," she said. "They can't get you in Sanctuary, either."

"Yeah. Unless, you know, I get *grabbed by some invisible force and dragged over the border*." I gave her the Look.

Gem shrugged. "We won't go near the border."

"Gem, I'm not going back to Sanctuary."

"Sure you are!" She shooed me forward as the line moved. "You're a Traveller. You won't be able to live without it."

"I'm serious! I can't go back there! I practically signed my soul away to something that's probably evil, and *I nearly died*. I'm not going back!" I detached myself from her and turned away.

Gemma ducked around to meet me. "Edge, dear, I'm quite serious." Her tone was light, but she stared into my eyes like she was searching out a sickness. "You won't be able to stay away from Sanctuary. You almost literally do not have a choice in the matter."

I froze. "What do you mean, I don't have a choice?"

Gem shrugged. "You're a Traveller. It gets in your blood. You think you don't want to go back now, but the crossing is addictive—*Sanctuary* is addictive. You'll go back. You might not want to, but you will."

My mind whirled in circles as I tried to digest the weight of what she'd said. Addictive? I was scared, and more than a little annoyed at Quoise for not warning me before teaching me to cross.

"Hey, you okay?" Gem asked, bumping me with her hip.

"What? Oh, yeah." I stretched a thin smile into place. "I'm fine."

She nodded decisively. "Good. I'd hate to have to murder Scott or something just to make you smile again." She grinned wickedly, eyes sparkling.

"You're incorrigible, you know that?"

"Thanks. I've never been so complimented in my entire life."

I shook my head, darkness still heavy in my chest. But as we clambered onto the bus and Gem slid into the seat next to me, my tension eased a tiny bit. Having Gem as an ally made the shadows a little less dark after all.

12

A COUPLE OF hours later, I lay stretched out on my bed, watching Gem hunch in the middle of the floor. She'd decided that her toenails needed immediate attention, and after bemoaning my complete lack of supplies, had found a kindred spirit in Anna, who'd let Gem help herself to whatever she wanted—something she'd die before letting me do, as I'd noted to both of them.

I closed my eyes and rested on my folded arms, but I couldn't get comfortable. Something niggled in the back of my mind, something I'd been meaning to say, but hadn't. Scrunching my lips to one side, I surveyed the room. My wardrobe door stood ajar, blocked by my schoolbag. My pencil case poked out the top.

I propped myself up. That was it. "Gem, there's something weird about my pen."

"Mm hmm."

I twisted around to snag the pencil case and dug out the pen. I stared at the pen's translucent emerald casing. It wasn't anything I could immediately spot, but there was definitely something off about it.

"Bummer." Gem screwed up her nose. "Tissue? I smudged."

I plucked a tissue from the bedside table and threw it at her. She caught it as it floated down and glanced at my pen. "Looks fine to me."

I frowned, turning it over in my hands. "No," I said. "There's definitely something different about it. It feels..." I trailed off, unable to find the words.

Gem shrugged. "Scott had it. Of course it's going to feel weird. It's probably covered in his mutant DNA. Oh, urgh." She shuddered.

I giggled. "I thought you didn't mind him."

"What, Scott?" She stared up at me, shocked. "The hideous cretin who keeps tormenting my best friend? No way. I mean, he's gorgeous, and charming, and I suspect much smarter than he lets on, and did I mention gorgeous? But no. Just, no. Not after how he's harassed you."

I grinned, somehow relieved to know that Gem had my back on that one.

"Actually," Gem said, straightening. "It might be mutant DNA. Close your eyes."

"What?" I wrinkled my brow at her.

"The pen! Close your eyes."

I did.

"What can you see?"

My heart leapt. "Black."

Gem huffed. "Well duh, your eyes are closed. I mean with your Road Mastery."

I shook my head. "No, that's what I mean. The pen's black, it has a print, or is covered in one, or something, and it's all black."

Gem was silent, and I opened my eyes to find her staring at me, lips twisted. "Don't... take this the wrong way or anything," she said after a moment. "It's not like I know how Road Mastery works or anything. But are you sure? I mean, black on black? Definitely?

I shook my head. "It's a different black. Promise."

Gem shrugged again. "Sure. So, what's it mean?"

I flopped back on my bed. "*I* have no idea, how am I supposed to know?"

"You're the Road Master."

"And you're the one who's been visiting Sanctuary since you were born." I stuck my tongue out at her. "Gem, seriously: I found out about this *last week*. One weekend does not an expert make."

I closed my eyes again, and colours swirled in the darkness.

"It's so weird," I said eventually. "It's like all of a sudden I'm a different person. I can do all this stuff and I didn't even know it existed a week ago. What will I find out *next* week?"

"Pigs fly?"

I rolled over and pulled a face at Gem. "Ah ha. Funny. I'm so glad you're taking me seriously. It's not like I'm having an identity crisis over here or anything. Thanks."

Gem sighed and recapped the nail polish. "Em, I know you think you're being serious when you say you're not going back to Sanctuary, but please trust me on this: you won't be able to not go. You know how calm everything is when you're there. Sooner or later you're going to get stressed out by school or Scott or the end of the world, and you'll know: the best way to destress is Sanctuary. You won't be able to help yourself."

I opened my mouth to protest but she waved me quiet.

"I'm serious. It's just the way it works. Once you know you can travel, you can't *not* travel, just like with your Road Mastery. Now you know you have it, you can't not see it."

I buried my face in my pillow. "I hate you."

"What?" she chirped. "I can't hear your insults clearly."

I sat up and threw the pillow at her. She squeaked, waving her feet in the air. "Wet! Polish!"

"I hate you," I said, ignoring her theatrics. "Because you're right. And I don't *want* you to be right, and I hate that you're right, and maybe someday I will go back to Sanctuary, but not yet, okay? Not soon."

Gem nodded. "Sure. I know. The shadow thing was horrific."

I flopped backwards on the bed, miserable. It wasn't just the shadows and the fact that they'd tried to eat me. What Gem had said earlier in the day was right: the shadows were hardly likely to get me in Sanctuary unless I strayed too close to the border, and there was exactly zero chance of *that* happening again. I grabbed my other pillow and smooshed it over my face.

"It's not just that," I mumbled. I didn't want to tell Gemma what had happened, didn't want to repeat and relive, but I knew that until I told *someone* here in Nowra what had happened, why I'd come here in the first place, it could never be my home. And I wanted to go back to Melbourne, of course I did... But Gemma was pretty cool. Maybe she deserved the whole truth after all.

I peeked out from under the pillow and saw Gem staring intently at me, hugging one leg to her chest with her chin resting on her knee.

I sighed and let the pillow flop back over my face. "There's more," I told it, staring at the pattern of light and dark where the stuffing filled it unevenly. "It's not just the thing with the shadows. That... Well, to be honest, it kind of feels like a dream now. A bad, scary, stupid dream, but a dream. It was too farfetched, too unreal, and it's like my brain's just stuck it in the 'imaginary' box and is trying to move on." I blinked a few times, feeling my eyelashes drag against the pillow cover and wondering how to say what needed to be said.

"November," I said after a moment. "My life ended in November." To Gem's credit, she neither laughed, nor made zombie comments.

My insides writhed and I squirmed. I gave up and flipped over, hanging my head and one arm off the edge of the bed.

"Dad had to go to court," I mumbled into the blanket. "He saw some drug lord doing a deal, or something. I don't know exactly. He wouldn't tell us. But the police called him, they wanted him to help them."

The momentum built, and all of a sudden the story was rushing out, uncontrollable.

"He didn't want to, said he knew it would get us all into trouble, but the police kept asking and asking and then there was this murder, someone from Anna's school. She didn't really know the girl but it freaked her out because the girl... Well, she *looked* like Anna. I know. I found her. In the bathroom at the train station, with one side of her face smashed in."

I took a deep, shaky breath. "So. Anna told Dad that if the morons were going to come after us anyway, he should definitely testify against them and get them locked up. So, he did. And the guy was found guilty of a whole bunch of stuff, though they never managed to pin the murder on anyone, and then we thought everything was okay, but then we started getting letters in the post. That *really* freaked us out, because one girl had already died, and if they knew where we lived..."

I shrugged, the old fear itching at my neck. "So we reported it to the police, of course, and all of a sudden..."

I gasped against a sudden sob that threatened to surface. "Then all of a sudden, we were leaving Melbourne, and on Friday I told my friends we were going, but I couldn't tell them where or why, and then Monday I was here in Nowra, with no friends, and no home, and no life."

I pressed my face against the blanket, trying to stifle the tears. I missed my old home so much my chest ached and my eyes burned. I wanted to crawl into the pile of cushions I'd had in my bedroom back in Melbourne, snuggle up in the sun, and go to sleep so I could wake up and realise this had all been a horrible, horrible dream.

Gem worked a wad of tissues between my damp, snotty face and the blanket. "Wow," she said softly.

I pressed the tissues against my eyes and breathed deeply before rolling over and staring at the roof. "Yeah. Wow, right?"

She crawled onto the bed next to me and pulled me onto her lap. "No wonder you're jumpy," she said, stroking my hair.

I scowled. "Yeah, well, you would be too if evil shadows had just tried to devour you, drug lords and criminals aside."

Gem was silent as her fingers worked through my hair, braiding and plaiting and then twisting it all together. I closed my eyes and let the rhythmic motion soothe me.

When she was done, she shifted under my shoulders. "We have to figure this out."

My stomach jolted. "Why?"

"Because you're not going to settle until we do."

I scrunched up my face. "I'm fine."

"You're not fine. You're tense and jumpy and I want you to come back to Sanctuary with me. I've wanted a friend to share it with as long as I can remember. Besides," she said, wriggling out from under me. "You promised to help."

I groaned, shrugging my shoulders up around my ears. "Can't we wait? Like, maybe just for a week or something?"

Gem considered me. "Will waiting help?"

I opened my mouth to tell her that of course it would—and stopped. I sighed as visions of bulging shadows filled my mind. "Probably not."

"So let's go then."

"What, *now*?" I sat up.

"The sooner we go, the sooner we can figure out what's going on, and the sooner you'll feel better," Gem said.

I stared at her, incredulous. "It's nine o'clock at night! And we're thirteen! What if we *can't* figure it out, did that occur to you?"

Gemma grinned. "No."

"Argh!" I threw another pillow at her. "Incorrigible!"

Gem put a finger to her chin in mock thought. "Hmm, you know, I think you've said that before."

My heart hammered in my chest. How was I going to convince Gem not to go? "But... it's dark!"

"It's just dark," she said. "This is Earth, not Sanctuary."

I shook my head. "No, I didn't mean that. I mean... It's late." Quite besides anything else, the parentals would have a fit if I decided I wanted to go wandering around at this hour.

"And?"

Frogging elephants, she sounded genuinely puzzled. "I have parents, Gemma," I said with exaggerated slowness. "They take care of me. This means they do things like make *rules*."

She wrinkled her brow, perplexed. "You're not allowed out after dark?"

I nodded.

She nearly had a kitten right there on the rug, gasping with silent laughter and holding her ribs.

I rolled my eyes. "Yes, Gem. I'm not allowed out after dark, by myself, in the wild."

"It's the clearing!" Gem gasped. "And you're not alone, you're with me."

"Yes, but there might be thugs," I explained patiently, ignoring the way my chest clenched when she mentioned the clearing. "Or child molesters. Or people doing drug deals they didn't want anyone to witness and if we saw them they might, you know, hunt us down and murder us. That kind of thing."

"Indeed," she said, twitching her eyebrows.

I rolled my eyes again and took her hand. "I know this is a confusing topic," I said, patting the back of her hand. "I'm trying to make it easy for you. My parents are the kind that believe in all the scary stuff that can happen to Children Our Age. There's no way they'll let me go down to the clearing at this time of night."

And of course, it was not totally, utterly, one-hundred percent convenient to blame my reluctance on them. Not at all.

"My parents *know* the kind of stuff that can happen to 'Children Our Age'," Gemma said, taking her hand back. "And they let me out."

"Your parents are special."

"Well, you're not going to sleep until we figure this out."

"I'm not going to sleep if I get abducted by shadows again, either." I tried the Look again.

Unmoved, Gem waved her hand dismissively. "Highly unlikely."

She was worse than Veve with a ball. Maybe we could find a compromise. "Well..." I said, not sure how Gem would receive my idea. "There is *one* thing we could do..."

Gem raised an eyebrow. "Seriously?"

My mouth went dry. I swallowed until my tongue remembered how to work, then stood, rubbing at my arms. "Why do you want to go to the clearing, precisely?"

Gem shrugged. "To see these creepy shadows of yours, I guess."

I scowled. "They're not my shadows."

"Sorry, I know—"

I dismissed her apology with a wave. "We don't have to go to the clearing to see the shadows," I said. "There are some in the yard."

Gem bolted upright. "What, your yard?"

I nodded.

"Really?"

I nodded again.

"Golly. No wonder you're jumpy. *Really*." She shook her head. "Well then." She scrambled off the bed and headed to my wardrobe, where she scuffled around in the mess for a moment. "Shoes," she said, holding out my sneakers.

Obediently, I slipped them on, watching as she laced up her own.

"Jacket?"

I giggled.

"What?" Gem put her hands on her hips. "It's cool out there!"

"You sound like Mum."

She made an exasperated noise and helped herself to my wardrobe again, pulling out my denim jacket for herself and the cotton trench coat for me. "Come on," she said, buttoning herself up. "Let's skedaddle."

I giggled again, full of nerves. For crying out loud, we were only going to the backyard. I forced myself to sober. "Okay. Ready."

Gem eased the door open and peered out into the hallway. The TV blared in the living room, and I could hear the thump-thump bass of what passed for music in Anna's room. "All clear."

I stuffed my pen into my pocket. "Let's go."

We tiptoed down the hall to the laundry and opened the door, jumping when it creaked louder than Dad's deepest snores. We darted through, closed the door, and fell against it not-giggling—the silent, uncontrollable shaking that happens when you're trying so hard not to laugh that it makes whatever you're not laughing at fifty times funnier.

Yeah. Us. Very sensible girls.

A creak in the hallway snapped us back to sanity and in a frantic flurry we tumbled out into the yard. We clung to each other, breathing quickly.

"Do you think they heard us?" I managed.

Gem shook her head, lips pressed tightly together.

Something crashed into the back of us and we screamed. My heart pounded as I twisted around and caught Veve by the collar. She barked, just once. We gasped and took a moment to regain our breath—and our normal heart rates.

"Veve you beast, you nearly killed us!" I said. "Are you *trying* to get us caught?"

"We're only in the yard," Gem pointed out. "It's not like you're sneaking out or anything."

I nodded, but the unease had returned, clinging to my shoulders like a too-tight shirt. "C'mon," I muttered. "This way." I led Gem around to where the horrible spiky bushes lurked against the side fence. They were about half my height again, all gnarled branches and inch-long thorns, with long, serrated leaves. Mum had been on at Dad to get rid of them since we'd arrived, but for whatever reason, he kept delaying.

I shuddered at the blackness oozing out of them. "They're awful."

"Hmm," Gem said, twisted her lips and tapping a finger against her chin. "I see what you mean."

I turned away, marvelling at how cool and collected Gem appeared. I could barely stand to look at the horrible shadows; the sense of *wrong* emanating from them was almost tangible.

"Well," Gem said. "That's interesting."

"That's one way of putting it," I muttered. "So, why do you think they're here?"

Gem screwed up her nose. "I think... Eh, really, I can't remember a hundred percent. I need to ask Quoise."

"Well, what can you remember?"

She sighed. "It's to do with the way the dimensions are folded," she said. "Did the fairies tell you about that?"

I shook my head. "Kind of."

"It's like..." Gem waved her hands in the dim light. "Imagine crumpling some sheets of paper."

"How many?"

"I don't know, as many as you like!" Gem flapped her hands. "One for every dimension."

"I don't own that much paper." I was being persnickety and I knew it, but it was better than letting the darkness get to me.

"Edge! Stop it." She peered at me to make sure that I had. "So, you crumple up some sheets of paper, then smooth them out again and stack them on top of each other. Because they're crumpled still, they don't touch each other perfectly, right? They only touch in places."

"And that's our world touching Sanctuary and all the other dimensions?"

"Well, our world only touches Sanctuary. All of the worlds do, Sanctuary is the... I don't know, the central train station. But yes, you can get to all of Sanctuary's different dimensions."

I stared at the blacker-than-black under the bushes. "So that's..." I swallowed. "You're telling me I have a portal to the Valley in my backyard."

Gem nodded. "I think so."

My hands tightened to fists. I forced myself to unclench my fingers one by one. "Great. Just when I thought I was safe." I shook my head. "But why here? The Valley is..." I did some quick calculations in my head. "The Valley is east of Sanctuary, and we're west of the clearing right now."

"Crumpled paper. Only more twisted. It doesn't match up one for one, and distances between them are skewed. The clearing's what, ten minutes from here? But if we travelled over here"—she gestured at the bushes—"we might come out half an hour away, or an hour, or right next to it."

I ran my hands over my face. "I think my brain is leaking out my ears."

Veve bumped into my leg and I squatted beside her, running her tail through my fingers. "Are you done?" I asked. "Can we go inside now?"

"Edge!" She huffed in exasperation. "We haven't figured anything out yet!"

I burrowed my fingers through Veve's ruff. "Well we're hardly going to, standing in the yard staring at shadows and bushes. It's not like we're going to travel through them."

129

Gem tapped her chin again. "The question is, though, why can we see them at all? Your brain isn't the only thing that's leaking, methinks."

"That's lovely," I said, pressing my cheek against Veve's shoulder, which stank like dog but was at least warm and alive.

Gem began pacing. "I need to ask Quoise. Not that she'll tell me anything, although if any fairy was going to, she would. The Valley is definitely leaking, or expanding, or something."

"The clearing's still fine, though," I said.

Gem shook her head. "For now. But then again, maybe not. How do we know if the clearing is shadow-free all the time? These shadows aren't here all the time, are they?"

I shook my head, stomach dropping as I recalled the first time I'd been to the clearing, when I'd seen horrible shadows lurking in the trees on the Sanctuary side of the creek.

I'd thought the glade was safe, but apparently nowhere was.

"We should go and look."

"What?" I jerked my head up.

"We have to go to the clearing."

"I thought we established that I'm not allowed."

"I didn't say we should ask permission."

My pulse skipped at her serious expression. "You..." I stopped and cleared my throat. "You want me to sneak out?"

Gem shrugged, trying—and failing—to hide a grin. "You want to sleep tonight or not?"

I gaped some more. I never broke the rules or pushed the boundaries. That was something Anna did, not me. Anna was headstrong and independent; I was guilty. Even if I hadn't done anything wrong, my parents only had to quirk an eyebrow at me and I felt weighed down by guilt. "I won't sleep if I get snatched into the Valley!"

"I promise, we won't go near the other side. We'll just stand right near the tunnel and look." She grinned beatifically.

"No," I said flatly. "I'm not going." Veve wriggled, knocking me over, and I sat on the grass and pulled her into my lap.

"But Edge—"

Gem bent to sit.

Without warning, Veve exploded into snarls and shot toward the prickly bushes.

I may or may not have squeaked. Gem definitely did, landing butt-first, sprawled on the ground. "Veve! I'm going to wring your hairy neck!"

Just as suddenly, Veve's barking stopped. The silence pressed down, too loud, too full.

"Gem," I whispered. "Are you all right?"

"Yes," she whispered back. "Are you?"

"Yes. Can you see Veve?" Because all of a sudden, my heart was pounding. Not only was the silence too loud, but the darkness was too complete, and although I should easily have been able to make out Veve's silhouette with the residual light from the house, I couldn't see a thing.

I sensed more than saw Gem roll over and crawl toward the bushes. My Road Master sense prickled. "Gem, I think we should go back inside."

"Just a second." She crawled forward. "I want to find that dog and pluck the hairs off her tail. I'm covered in mud and filth."

The darkness shifted. I grabbed at her foot and missed. "The shadows," I hissed as blacker-than-black shadows bulged in the darkness. My heart pounded. "Gemma, we have to go. The shadows are wrong."

Silence.

"Gem?"

The darkness bore down on me.

"Gemma? Veve?"

Silence, heavy and thick.

My skin crawled and I breathed quickly, my chest tight with dread. "Gemma? Gem, this isn't funny! Answer me!"

I flailed forward in the darkness, waving my arms where Gemma had been crouching.

Nothing.

I froze as images of what I might run into instead multiplied in my mind. Panic wrapped a tight band around my chest and I thought the skin over my spine might writhe off my back.

"Veve!" I called hoarsely. "Here, puppy!"

More silence. No bark, friendly or otherwise, no brush of fur against my leg.

Something tickled my neck and I screamed, then realised it was a moth.

Gone. Gem and Veve, both gone.

Frantically, I scrabbled back from the bushes.

Shadows, in my own yard. That wasn't fair. I hadn't gone anywhere, I hadn't done anything. This was my *own yard*. I was *supposed* to be here.

Wind gusted across the yard and the hair on the back of my neck prickled. The Valley. Streaming out from the horrible bushes and not-right shadows, the cloying, sickly-sweet smell of the Valley.

I needed Quoise. She'd know what to do, and I couldn't just abandon Gem and Veve. I needed help.

The creek. Frog it all, I was going to have to go down to the clearing and travel across to Sanctuary.

Biting back tears, I headed back to the house. Thank heavens I'd taken to storing my seed packet in the laundry.

My heart hammered. Why had the shadows snatched them like that? They hadn't done any magic at all, let alone death magic. Could a dog even offer a death sacrifice? Morbidly, I imagined Veve stepping on a bug at a crucial moment.

Stupid. It didn't work like that. At the back door, I gritted my teeth. Gemma owed me big time for this. If she hadn't been so stupidly interested in 'solving the mystery', we'd still be inside painting toenails and discussing green pens. I blinked back my tears, snuck into the laundry, grabbed my seeds from the cupboard, and jumped out of my skin. "Anna," I gasped at the head poking into the room.

She raised an eyebrow. "It's twenty past nine. What on earth are you doing?"

"Um, playing with Veve?" My pulse screamed in my ears. *Please, you have to let me go. The Valley has them. I have to get help.*

"And you need seeds because...?" Anna stared pointedly at the packet in my hand.

"Um, we're playing a game?" *Please, Anna. Please!*

Anna rolled her eyes. "Let me guess. It's a game in the clearing by the creek?"

I shuffled. "Maybe?"

Anna sighed. "You and your guerrilla gardening. At least tell me you're taking the dog."

I hesitated before nodding. I mean, technically I wasn't going anywhere Veve wasn't, right? So I was sort of taking the dog...

Anna nodded. "Good. Though why you had to decide to revel in our almost-freedom at this time of night I'll never know."

I shrugged and tried to smile.

"Have you got your phone?"

I patted my pocket. "Yup."

"Be home by midnight, okay?" Anna said. "If you're caught, we never had this conversation, or I swear I'll get you in so much trouble you'll never go anywhere but school until you're fifty."

"Fifty-year-olds don't go to school."

"Try me," she said darkly, and disappeared.

Relief flooded through me. Anna was good to her word; she wouldn't rat me out.

I headed down the street to the gravel path through the boulders. The moon hadn't risen and the sky seemed darker than usual. I checked quickly with my Road Mastery and couldn't sense anything amiss, but it still sent a shiver down my spine.

At the bottom of the path, panic fluttered around the edges of my consciousness. Down here, even the stars seemed faint, and even though my Road Mastery told me nothing unusual was around, the shadows everywhere seemed too dark, too deep, too sharp to be quite real. Nerves thrilled through my stomach as I ducked under an overgrown eucalypt branch that hung over the path. "It's fine," I muttered. "It's just a perfectly normal tree."

But out of the corner of my eyes, I kept watch: if a tree tried to grab me, I'd be ready for it. Impulsively I picked up a long stick from the side of the path. *Take that, trees*, I thought. *Wood against wood.* If only I had something to use against the shadows.

I reached the scrappy tunnel all my travels through to the clearing had made, and hesitated. *Frogging elephants*, I thought, wanting so badly to press my eyes closed but terrified of what might happen if I did. I swallowed, scrubbing my sweaty palms against my jeans. Frogging elephants.

Trees, shadows...

I exhaled firmly and set my shoulders. This was not negotiable. My best-and-only friend was in danger, and so was my dog. This wasn't about the rules, or even being scared. This was about not letting the shadows win.

I marched into the tunnel, definitely not holding my breath and certainly not flicking nervous glances all around at the shadowy darkness. I would cross to Sanctuary, find Quoise, and she would have a plan to rescue them.

Everything was going to be just fine.

The shadows across the creek weren't at all darker than normal, tendrils of blackness drifting toward me, reaching, whispering things just beyond hearing. Of course not.

I crossed to Sanctuary, faster than I'd ever crossed before. Quoise had better have a plan.

13

I TUMBLED INTO Sanctuary already sprinting. "Quoise!" I shouted as I ran up the slope. "Quoise!" My breath caught in my throat and I slowed. "Quoise!" I called again.

Throat burning, I stumbled to a halt outside the stables, steadying myself against the wall and leaning over my knees. I gasped and swallowed, gasped and swallowed, and my heart rate began to settle. I seriously needed to be fitter if I was going to have to run for my life this often.

I straightened and looked around, chest still heaving but no longer on fire. The soft glow of Sanctuary enveloped me and a gentle breeze brought with it the scent of jasmine and salt water.

I'd never realised before how overtly calming Sanctuary was. Gemma was right; it was totally infectious. But I shook my head and started up the slope toward the Lodge. I needed my adrenaline. Much as might hate it, I had the strong suspicion that tonight would include another trip into the Valley. Nerves fluttered in my stomach as I entered the Lodge's main entrance for the first time.

I stared. There was a whole lot of fluttering going on in here, but none of it was due to my stomach. Scores of fairies, maybe even hundreds, flittered around the vast room, some darting quickly, some wafting gently, all a riot of shimmer and glimmer and colour.

A gold-winged fairy noticed me and darted over, hovering at eye level. "Can I help you?"

"I'm looking for Quoise, please," I said. "It's urgent."

She smiled. "Just a moment."

She left and I jittered, shifting from foot to foot and wondering if Gem and Veve were okay, if they'd been devoured by the shadows, and how on earth the shadows had reached across to grab them. Only the power of a death sacrifice was supposed to allow a person to travel into the Valley.

Yet I'd been drawn across by a mysterious green-and-gold stranger, and now Gem and Veve had been taken. I scrunched up my face, trying to remember if there had been any trace of green or gold, any smell of mint in the air when they'd disappeared.

I couldn't remember a thing. One second they'd been there, and then they hadn't.

I clenched my fists in frustration. Shadows behaving strangely, both here in Sanctuary and on Earth. People getting sucked into the Valley for no apparent reason. After I'd pointed out where the shadows were coming from, Gem had said it was like the Valley was leaking, darkness oozing out everywhere it touched.

And, I thought, sticking my hands into my pockets and rediscovering my pen, traces of darkness all over stationary Scott had stolen.

I let my subconscious ponder over that for a while, and was startled when it handed me a memory of a task we'd done in geography at the end of last year. We'd had to do mapping work showing the suburbs where we lived. I hadn't known the area well enough to it to register at the time, but Scott's had been just a little way down from the school—right across the creek from the clearing.

Of course, it might not mean anything, but what were the chances of that? I snorted, realised I was chewing my thumbnail, and shook my hand.

Somehow, this was all connected, and I was beginning to suspect that a certain irritating boy might be the link. If Gem and Veve didn't escape this whole episode intact, I might just have to wring his neck.

"Hello?" The gold-winged fairy had returned and was smiling apologetically. "I'm sorry, but you just missed her. She's gone down to check on the foals."

I screamed internally. How had I missed her? I'd just *come* from there. My best friend was missing, dragged into the valley of death sacrifices and all things evil, and I was stuck playing the physical equivalent of phone tag. Doing my best not to glare, I nodded my thanks and left the hall.

This time as I stalked back down the slope I was in no danger of losing my adrenaline rush to Sanctuary's calming effects. I was certain: Scott was involved in all this, and when I found out how, he was going to pay.

I ducked inside the stables, calling out as I did. "Quoise?" Relief flooded over me as I sensed her inside.

"Edge, is that you?"

Quoise would know what to do. "Yes, it's me."

Wings fluttered in the dimness, then light flared and Quoise balanced on the rail near me, hand glowing brightly. "Come to see the foals?" she asked. "They're doing so well considering." She shook her head.

"Yes, it's very sad," I said quickly. "But I'm here about Gemma. She's missing."

Concern flitted across Quoise's face. "Oh well," she said, brushing it away. "There are lots of places she could be. I'm sure everything's fine."

I shook my head. "No. We were in the backyard together—it was dark, it's nearly ten at home—and she just... disappeared. Veve too."

Quoise relaxed into a smile. "Oh, well, maybe a new portal has opened in your yard. That happens sometimes. She probably just travelled over and is hiding here somewhere."

I met Quoise's gaze willing her to understand how serious this was. "She... she did travel. But she didn't travel into Sanctuary. The creepy shadows are in my yard."

Quoise paled. "Gemma offered death?" she said hoarsely.

"No." I shook my head quickly. "No. Something dragged her across." Goosebumps rose on my arms as I remembered stumbling in the darkness, arms reaching for a person that suddenly wasn't there.

"You have to look for her, send out a search party or something," I said, tripping over my words. "You have to go, someone has to find her, you have to, please..."

I squeezed my eyes shut against the tears. *I don't want to go back there.*

"Oh, Edge," Quoise said softly. "We can't."

My stomach lurched. "What do you mean? You're a fairy! You're magical! You have to help!"

She shook her head. "We can't travel into the Valley. Fairies are creatures of Sanctuary, we're born of its magic. Fairies are life, Edge, and we can only exist where there is life magic."

"But things live in the Valley. There are trees, and there's grass, and..." I strangled a sob.

She landed gently on my shoulder and hugged my neck. "You know they're not really alive," she whispered. "I'm sorry. I can't go."

I took a second to collect myself. I'd suspected all along that I'd have to go in and look for Gem. This didn't change anything. "Okay," I said, taking a steadying breath. "Okay. So I'm going in alone."

Quoise spiralled into the air. "What? Edge, you can't cross the border! You'll die!"

Guilt tugged at me. "I survived last time." *Barely*.

"Only just!" Quoise said, echoing my thoughts.

"Do you have a better alternative?" I raised my voice. "She's my best friend, Quoise! Veve is my dog! I *have* to save them."

Quoise shook her head. "Edge, that's all very admirable, but you can't cross over. I can't honestly believe you got out of there *once*, let alone tempting fate a second time. And even if you can somehow survive, you've no idea where they might be, if it's not already too late. This is the Valley we're talking about here, not some fairground or a picnic."

"I *know* that!" I said, scrubbing my hands through my hair. "But I survived last time, so why can't I try again?"

"Because you can't!" Quoise shouted. Instantly she recoiled, as though shocked by her own volume. "I'm sorry. But you just can't."

Anna's voice rang in my head. *Don't you ever get sick of 'just because'?* I took a deep breath, focusing on

142

calming myself. "I survived last time," I said, quieter. "Please. They're my friends. I have to try." Anna was right: this time, 'just because' wasn't good enough.

Quoise stared at me for a long moment, then sighed and fluttered away.

I held my breath, wondering if that was the best I could expect, but she returned and landed on the rail again, holding a wiry, cream rope.

"Take this, then," she said, offering it to me.

"What is it?" I asked, reaching out to accept.

"Unicorn hair. They're the only creatures who can cross the border safely; they belong equally to life and death. I'm not sure what it can do for you once you're in the Valley, but at least it'll get you across. Despite what happened last time, you can't actually waltz across the border like it's not there.

"And if the other fairies hear about this and you get banned from Sanctuary, don't come crying to me. Rules exist *for a reason*."

"I didn't waltz across," I snapped as I took the unicorn hair. "Something dragged me. And I know all about the reasons why rules exist," I added, stomach heaving. Georgia's blood plastered across tiles in a train station bathroom were all well and good, but this time, if I *didn't* break the rules, it could be Gemma's blood plastered all over the ground. It was slowly starting to dawn on me that maybe, just maybe, the way to defeat evil wasn't to play nicely by the rules and ignore it. Some things you had to stand up for. After all, wasn't that what Dad had done in the first place, testifying against that mob boss?

Hmm. That probably bore further examination, later, when Gem and Veve were safe. Somewhat distractedly, I lifted the unicorn hair to my face and sniffed, not really sure what I was doing or why. Mint. My stomach fluttered.

"What is it?" Quoise peered at me in concern.

Mint. To my Road Mastery, the unicorn smelled like mint, and mint had dragged me across. But she'd been missing for a week. "Unicorns should be able to cross, you say?"

Quoise nodded, concern shifting to confusion.

My subconscious dredged up another memory: Scott, outside the bathrooms as he'd handed me my pen. He'd told me my friend was okay. He couldn't have meant the unicorn, could he?

But at least it seemed that the one who'd dragged me into the Valley was benevolent, and not after my skin. I hadn't sold my soul to an insubstantial devil after all. I laughed. "I think," I said, shaking my head and stooping to tie the unicorn hair to my ankle, "that I might just be very all right. All things considered, anyway."

Quoise nodded. "Well then. Good luck, Emma Tanning. Come back again. If anyone can do it, it's probably going to be you."

I straightened and saluted. "Aye-aye, Quoise," I said. "I will."

Quoise took me to another little door behind vines like the one Gem had shown me. "We're boarding this up tomorrow," she said. "So don't think about sneaking through again."

I nodded, wondering how many of these there were, and if Gem's would be boarded up too. I couldn't voice exactly how much I never wanted to see the Valley again, or I'd turn and run—and she probably wouldn't have believed me anyway.

"Now," she said as I ducked into the passage, "I'll make sure that the other corridor is clear. You just... hurry. And be safe." She hesitated, then threw herself at me, hugging my neck. "Be careful."

"I will," I said, detaching her gently.

This passageway felt longer than Gemma's one, but eventually I crossed through the magical screen—the hallway had been empty, as Quoise had promised—and stood before the border.

I shuddered. The last time I'd been here, I'd nearly been lost to the Valley forever. This place was ridiculously dangerous, and forbidden for good reason. But Gem was my friend and Veve was my dog. I had to get them back.

And now, I thought, glancing down to where the unicorn hair hid under my jeans, there was more: the mysterious connection between the missing unicorn and my sudden abduction into the Valley intrigued me. Could it really be that she was trapped in the Valley too? What had I done when I'd pulled her away from the blackness?

And of course, how did Scott fit into everything?

I steeled myself and stepped into the shadows. There'd be time for questions later.

Nothing happened. I'd half expected to be dragged like last time, or to feel at least a tug, or a rush in my stomach—something to indicate I'd crossed into the land of death. Instead, I felt... nothing. And that creeped me out more than anything, because when I blinked, I got the sinking feeling that the reason the border was letting me through so easily was because the power of the Valley was focused elsewhere.

I shuddered. I had to hurry.

I gave Sanctuary one last wistful glance and walked farther into the Valley, trembling so hard I thought I might fall. The trees at least seemed to have forgotten our last meeting—or perhaps they'd only objected to my departure, not my presence. Well, I wasn't planning on leaving this time until I found Gem and Veve. One problem at a time.

I stepped forward and something stabbed me in the thigh. I jumped, but it was only my pen shifting.

I pulled it out and frowned. On this side of the border I didn't have to close my eyes to sense the darkness all over it. It was like being in the Valley amplified my Road Mastery even more than Sanctuary did—which was weird because everyone kept telling me that life magic was stronger.

I could definitely use it to my advantage, though. I hadn't really had a chance to test the limits of my Road Mastery yet, and anything that boosted it could only help me find Gem and Veve faster.

I closed my eyes, preparing to shut out all noise—and the horrible, abnormal silence of the Valley pressed in on me. I shuddered, feeling terribly exposed standing in the middle of dormant zombie trees with my eyes closed. I couldn't sense anything anyway, so I did the most logical thing—I followed the shadows. They weren't trying to devour me this time, but they still stretched oddly, streaming out from the heart of the Valley.

Every so often I closed my eyes to check in with my Road Mastery, but nothing appeared. My pace slowed and I sank into a tired daze. It was late back home after all. Must be getting close to midnight. What would Anna do if I wasn't back on time?

I stumbled. My pulse spiked for a moment, but the log I'd tripped on lay there, not reaching for me. I stared at it for half a minute before I realised I wasn't moving. I blinked and shook my head, but I was spent. I'd been walking for at least an hour.

Surely I could take a little break...

I sank to the ground and leaned against the log, staring vaguely into the distance. What had I been doing? The feeling that I'd forgotten something nagged in the back of my mind, but I was so tired, and I just needed to rest my eyes for a second.

A strange noise, just out of hearing, floated across the black behind my eyes. My name. It sounded like someone calling my name in smoky tones that promised the fulfilment of all my desires. I reached toward it, and the emptiness surrounded me, emptier than nothing, all wrapped up in the smell of overripe fruit and cold stone and fetid, rotting marshes.

"Sweet, so sweet... Come home... You are home... Sleep now, rest. So sweet..."

I closed my eyes, yawning.

"Yes, sleep so sweet, you are home, you are free. Do anything here, so sweet, you are free. Welcome home..."

Soft darkness fluttered along my limbs, imbuing them with power. Idly, I wondered if I could make the dead log at my feet turn green. I touched it. Darkness rippled along, leaving behind saturated green and budding leaves. I smiled sleepily. And people said the magic of life was stronger. I could do anything with death magic.

I cradled my head on my arm and a whisper drifted through the tendrils of darkness around me. *"Welcome,"* it crooned. *"Welcome home."*

14

I STRETCHED AWAKE, stiff and sore but feeling lazy and warm nonetheless. I opened my eyes and blinked at the trees around me. Since when did my room have trees in it?

I clambered to my feet and groaned as pain rang out on the inside of my skull. Wasn't I supposed to be doing something? I stared mindlessly at a landscape that probably wasn't my bedroom, but I couldn't remember what I'd been doing. Why had I decided to spend the night outside with weird trees that seemed to be frozen in the act of reaching for me?

Bizarre.

I should probably find someone, tell them I was here. A fragment of memory swam through my mental fog. Someone. I'd been looking for someone. That was right.

I screwed up my face, concentrating, trying to extract more from my memory.

Fear, panic. A bad place. Hmm. I strained for more, but a soft voice whispered to me. I couldn't catch the words, but it felt soothing, a dark, peaceful fog of nothingness, and my tension ebbed away again.

My ankle itched. I blinked as I lifted my jeans, surprised to discover some sort of strange rope tied around my ankle. I fumbled at it, wondering if I should remove it.

A breath of wind whispered against my face and I caught a faint trace of something minty. My frown deepened. None of the plants here looked anything like mint. It smelled nice, though, so I shrugged and smoothed my jeans down again.

Lacking anything better to do, I began to wander in the direction the wind had come from. The air dripped with humidity and I shrugged out of my jacket. It seemed like a heavy, clumsy thing to carry, so I left it lying on the ground.

Idly, I wondered what the time was. Out of habit I reached for my phone in my pocket. I wrinkled my nose. Flat battery. I shoved it back, wincing as something stabbed into my thigh.

I got a fleeting sense of déjà vu as I pulled out a green pen, but it was like trying to squeeze water. I growled in frustration and, for lack of anything better to do, kept walking.

The trees went on and on and on, one apparently-endless backdrop of sameness, and I'd just about given up hope of finding *anything* in this stupid wilderness when I stopped short. Was that a hoof print, there, in the mud?

I squatted. It was. I tilted my head. No wonder it had caught my eye; on certain angles it seemed to glow, a faint, pale green that gave the impression that fog had settled in it.

And, I realised, twitching my nose, something nearby smelled like mint.

"Right," I told the world at large. "That's it. What is going on?"

The same soft wind breathed against my face and connections whirled in my mind. A hoof print that smelled of mint, a disembodied voice, a strange rope around my ankle that might, I thought glancing at it, be made of horsehair. Was this who I was looking for?

"You! What are you *doing* here?"

I jumped at the first cry, and again as I swung around and saw who it was. "Scott!" Immediately I frowned. How had I known his name was Scott?

He looked as surprised as I felt. "I can't *believe* you! You ruin everything!"

"Yeah, I'm good at that," I said automatically, then frowned again. Why had I said that?

An image formed in my mind of this blond-haired boy called Scott surrounded by shadows, laughing on a cold mountaintop beneath the stars. Only, as I watched, the stars began to go out.

"But how did you even get here?" His question interrupted my vision and I blinked. "I don't see *you* having the guts to make the crossing."

My head sloshed. I had the distinct impression I'd just been about to remember something important—but it was gone. I shook my head again, then realised Scott was staring at me expectantly. "Sorry, what?"

He rolled his eyes. "Maybe you got dragged through. This place is leaking left, right and centre," he added under his breath.

Dragging. That rang a bell. Someone had been dragged somewhere, and I was supposed to be looking for someone. I sized Scott up. Was he the kind of person I would look for? The cold mountain flickered at the edges of my vision. Probably not.

I shoved my hands in my jeans pockets, thinking, and remembered that my pen was still there. I pulled it out and stared at it. It was connected to all this, somehow.

Scott made a strangled sort of noise. "Odd thing to carry around."

I shrugged. "Your fingerprints are on it." I blinked. My response had been instinctive again, but this time it had jarred some other thoughts loose too. I examined them. The pen had weird blackness all over it, but it wasn't black like the shadows I could sense following me, lurking just out of sight. Instead, it was black like Scott. Or at least, part of it was. Possibly it was black like both of them. I shook my head, brain-pretzelled.

Scott made an exasperated noise. "Ten points to the Princess. I was the one who gave it back to you and it has my fingerprints on it? Shocking, that."

I nodded absently. Fingerprints. I didn't think he meant the same thing by that as I did, but I couldn't quite grasp what I did mean.

Another fragment of memory filtered through. "Hang on. You did! You gave it back to me, and it was missing." I shook the pen at him, quizzical. "Did you steal it?"

Scott threw his hands up in the air. "I did not take your stupid pen! I found it for you, you stupid cow! I was trying to be nice to you, and you attacked me!" He turned and stomped away.

I wrinkled up my nose, trying to remember what he was talking about—and realised he had just called me a stupid cow. I marched after him. "Excuse me!" I said, poking him in the shoulder. "I am *not* a stupid cow. Although," I conceded as another wave of peaceful confusion rolled over me, "I may be stupid."

His face worked, trying on five different emotions at once, and at length he sighed. "Did you fall asleep?"

"Maybe."

He rolled his eyes. "You fell asleep. It's this place. It lulls you in. Unless it knows you're already on its side, it'll attack you if you try to leave and put you to sleep if you stay." He ran a hand over his head, tense. "You really do know how to ruin everything, don't you? If you'd just *listened* the first time I tried to tell you..."

"Tell me?!" I interrupted, mouth on autopilot again. "You never did anything but be a big, fat, stupid ass to me!" Not that I could remember a single thing about it, but apparently my subconscious knew how to hold a grudge well.

Scott cut me a filthy look. "Well nothing else was getting your attention, was it, McFrosty."

I shook my head. I had no details to fuel my case, but I knew he was wrong.

He stared at me for a moment longer, and when he spoke his voice was level and controlled. "Follow me." He stalked away.

"Where?" I said, crossing my arms.

"I'm getting you out," he said without turning. "And then I never want to see you here again."

Getting you out of here. The words echoed in my head, and more memory fragments slotted into place. I was here to get someone out. But who? I shrugged uncomfortably and followed Scott through the undergrowth.

At last Scott held up his hand to signal a halt, and I stopped gladly behind him. Humidity cloyed the air and although I'd become accustomed to the smell, I was dying for some water. My shirt was soaked through and sweat dripped down my legs inside the heavy denim of my jeans.

Scott glanced at me. "Ready then?"

I shrugged. "Sure." On top of the horrible humidity and my complete inability to remember why I was here, the place was deadly boring. The trees didn't move, the air didn't move, and besides the hoof print I'd seen earlier, we seemed to be the only things alive in the whole world.

"Okay," he said. "I'll have to travel with you, there's no way you can do it alone. You don't have the ability—or the guts." He glared briefly, daring me to challenge.

I shrugged, not really sure what he meant and abruptly too tired to argue.

"Stay behind me," he said, gesturing ahead to a small, greyish-white platform a couple of steps across. "When I say the word, put one hand on me." He tensed as though dreading the moment.

I couldn't say I blamed him; it wouldn't exactly be the highlight of my life, either.

"Whatever you do," he continued, "don't break contact with me."

I rolled my eyes at his melodrama but followed him as he headed toward the platform. My stomach skipped as I realised the greyish-white was bone. "Charming," I muttered.

"Okay," said Scott, ignoring me. "You stand there. And *don't move*."

I nodded and climbed into position.

Scott stepped up in front of me. He plunged his hands into his pocket and for an instant I thought that had been the signal, that I'd missed it and was going to be stuck in this horrible place alone.

I was so relieved when he pulled his hands out again that I almost didn't register the fact that he held a limp, white mouse in one hand and a pocketknife in the other.

Dread rippled over me and I gasped. *Death magic.* I couldn't remember what it was, didn't know how I knew what he was going to do—but I knew that it was bad. Blood drained from my face. "No."

"Put your hand on my back," Scott said quietly.

I did, pressing firmly to still my trembling. This was the only way out. I had to trust him.

"Close your eyes," he said softly.

I did.

His arms shifted.

The bottom dropped out of the world, and I screamed.

15

I SCREAMED AND I screamed, and still we fell, hurtling downwards so fast the air tore at my hair, my clothes, my skin. It hurt, frogging *elephants* it hurt, and it *would not stop*.

Then mercifully—finally—it did, leaving us sprawled on the ground under dark, shadowy trees, panting and gasping and wishing we could die.

Well, *I* wished I could die. Scott just scrambled to his feet and gave me contemptuous eyebrows. "Wuss," he said.

I may or may not have growled. "Why the frogging elephants did you not *warn* me that that was going to happen?"

"Would you have come if I had?"

"No!" I said, getting up and steadying myself against a tree trunk.

"Well, there you are then."

I stared about, trying to orient myself. "Where are we?"

Scott rolled his eyes. "You'll figure it out soon enough. That way, I think." He pointed to my left and I realised I could hear water trickling.

"Where are you going?"

Scott, heading the opposite way, paused. He opened his mouth, then stopped and shook his head. "Just go home," he said. "And don't come this way again, okay?" He disappeared through the trees, footsteps crackling in the dim light.

I sighed and headed toward the water. I broke out of the trees and reeled as memories slammed into place.

The creek. The clearing. *Veve. Gemma.*

My legs gave way and I crashed down into the water, crying out as rocks grazed my palms and memories battered my mind. What had I done?

Frogging elephants, I'd taken a *nap*. I buried my face in my hands, but I couldn't even cry. The failure was so incomprehensible, I couldn't do more than stumble around the edges of it.

Then fear stabbed through from another angle: Mum and Dad. What were they going to say? If they'd noticed I was missing they'd be going spare right now. I had to get home.

I struggled out of the stream, pulling my phone from my pocket. I glanced at it and winced. The cover was waterlogged, and even if the battery hadn't already run flat, I doubted I would have been able to turn it on. I shoved it back and hurried through the tunnel, relieved when I emerged on the other side to see that the sun was only just beginning to gild the treetops.

I forced myself to a jog, concentrating on my breathing—it helped block everything else out, and it was the only way to keep myself moving. I struggled against panic as I approached the house. What would my parents say? What would *Anna* say? Part of me wanted to turn around and march straight back to Sanctuary. I could look for Gem and Veve again and this time I'd find them, and we could hide in Sanctuary forever and be together and happy and not grounded for the rest of our lives. I didn't want to go to school till I was fifty.

I sighed. Even conveniently ignoring the fact that both of Gem's parents were Travellers, I didn't really mean it. I slipped through the back gate and constructed a cover story in my head.

By the time I reached the sliding door that led into the lounge room, I had it down pat. But as soon as I walked through the door, all excuses evaporated. Gem and Veve were gone.

Mum was in the kitchen, kneading bread dough. She raised an enquiring eyebrow at me as I entered. "You're up early. And you're soaking wet."

I nodded, dripping on the tiles and fighting the desire to run.

"Where's Gemma?"

I cringed, only half acting. "She went home."

"Home?" Mum's hands paused in the dough.

"She remembered that she needed some stuff for her history assignment today. But..." I tore my gaze from the floor and looked Mum in the eyes, my own prickling with tears I didn't need to fake. "But Mum, Veve's missing."

Concern flooded Mum's face and she paused with her hands in the dough. "Are you sure?"

I nodded. "We looked everywhere. I think... I think she must have got out the gate." I squeezed my eyes shut. *Please believe me...*

A rustle of cloth, soft footsteps. Mum hurried to the door and slid it open. "Veve!"

I shook my head. "She's not there, Mum." The tears spilled over. She might never be there again, and it was all my fault. I should have told Gemma no. "I even checked down at the creek. I can't find her anywhere."

Mum re-entered the house and scooped me into her arms, soggy clothes and all. "Don't worry," she said, squeezing me tight. "We'll find her. I'll print out some posters at work and ring all the local vets. Don't worry. She'll be okay."

I locked myself in my bedroom, turned on some music to muffle my voice, and sat on the floor, cradling the home phone. Anna had stuck my phone in a bowl of rice in an attempt to dry it out, hissing under her breath to me, "Don't think I don't know what time you didn't make it home last night."

That had made my stomach drop, but it was nothing to the call I now had to make. Mrs Caro needed to know what had happened. My chest tightened and I gripped the phone. I couldn't do it.

I *had* to do it. A sob strangled my throat and in a rush I dialled Gemma's number. She had to know.

The phone rang and rang. Mrs Caro had probably already left for work. I moved the phone away to hang up.

"Hello?"

I froze.

"Hello, who is it?"

I inched the phone back to my ear, a movement that took hours. "Hello," I rasped. I swallowed and tried again. "Hello. It's Emma here."

"Oh, Emma! Hello! What can I do for you? You can't be wanting to speak to Gemma, she's with you, isn't she?"

Tears leaked from my tightly closed eyes. *Just say it, Emma*, I told myself. *Now. Do it.* "No, Mrs Caro. No, she's not."

"I'm sorry?" Mrs Caro said. "Yes, just a minute dear, I'm speaking with Emma."

"Oh, if you need to go..." I said hurriedly, praying that she would.

"No, no, it's quite all right. Gemma's *not* with you, did you say?"

My stomach flip-flopped. "No. That's what I rang about. Gemma... She's... I mean, last night..."

I gasped back the tears, trying to keep myself under control. "Mrs Caro, she's in the Valley," I blurted. "I'm sorry," I choked. "I'm so sorry, I tried to find her but I couldn't, and I fell asleep and then Scott found me and took me home and I didn't even know what was happening, and she's missing and I couldn't find her and I forgot! I'm so, so sorry!"

"Emma, calm down," Mrs Caro said firmly. "The Valley? Why on earth would Gemma be in the Valley?"

"She was dragged there. Last night, in the—"

"Don't say anything more," Mrs Caro interrupted. "You're on your way to school?"

I nodded, wiping away tears. "I will be soon. Mum's going to drive me."

"Does she know?" Mrs Caro's voice sharpened.

"No," I replied. "Just that Veve is missing."

"Veve?"

"My dog. She's with Gemma."

"Oh. I'm sorry," Mrs Caro said softly. "Really, I am. But... Well, at least Gemma has someone with her, right?"

My voice came out as a hoarse whisper. "Right."

Mrs Caro resumed her business-like tone. "I'll come and get you as soon as I can. Does anyone else know Gemma is missing?"

"Quoise," I said. "She let me into the Valley."

"Quoise? Oh, well, I suppose that's good." She took a deep breath and exhaled slowly. "Okay. Emma, it's going to be okay, you hear me?"

"I'm sorry," I whispered.

"It's not your fault," she said. "Whatever happened, it's not your fault. Hang in there. I'll meet you as soon as I can." She hung up.

I stared at the phone as I scrubbed away a fresh wave of tears. I had to get ready for school. And then Mrs Caro would arrive and have some perfect solution, and everything would be fine.

I pulled my uniform on, pointedly ignoring the little voice in my head that told me I was thinking wishfully. Of course Mrs Caro would have a solution. Of course she would. I just had to wait and see what it was.

16

I ARRIVED AT school alternating between depression and electric tension, wondering when Mrs Caro would arrive. I hurried off to roll call, hoping she'd be there before first period. In the meantime, I sat at the back of the room, doodling in my school diary, mind racing as I brainstormed ways to rescue Gem.

I'd gotten exactly nowhere when the bell rang. Mrs Caro still hadn't appeared, so I gritted my teeth and headed to Maths, determined not to spend too long there.

I took my usual seat front and centre, and did my best to look as unwell as possible. It worked. Five minutes into class, I called Mr Morris over and told him I wasn't well. He took one look at me and sent me to sickbay. Turns out being stressed out of my mind had its uses.

I lay on the sickbay bed trying to rest, but my mind buzzed. When the nurse came in and told me Mrs Caro was here to pick me up, I nearly melted in relief—and then snapped tight as a bowstring, because if I was Mrs Caro and knew what had happened, I'd probably want to kill me right now.

I headed out to reception. Mrs Caro nodded and shepherded me out to the car without comment.

The heavy clouds broke as we buckled up, rain pattering down on the roof. I let it fill the silence until we pulled out of the car park and onto the main road.

"Mrs Caro," I said, twisting toward her, "I know you're probably mad as anything right now, but I have to go back to the Valley. I have to find her."

She nodded. "I know."

"You do?" I frowned. I'd expected her to try to talk me out of it, not agree straight up.

"Yes. But I have some questions for you first."

"Of course, anything." I stared at her, wondering how she could appear so calm. Her only daughter was trapped in the Valley, and here she was coolly indicating and sliding in and out of traffic like it was any ordinary day. There was only one logical explanation: underneath her normal, composed exterior, Mrs Caro was a superhero.

We drove out to the subdivision where the Caros lived and stopped right next to a vacant lot that provided easy access to the creek path.

"Your house is closer, but I don't want to risk you being seen by someone who knows you," Mrs Caro said, twisting around. "So. You went into the Valley to find her, is that right?"

I nodded, watching the rain spatter on the windscreen.

"The first and most important question then is, how did you get there?"

I peeled down my school sock to expose my ankle. "Quoise gave me unicorn hair." I hadn't been able to bear the thought of taking it off this morning, even if it did itch like mad sometimes.

Mrs Caro's face softened. "That was kind of her, especially considering their standard policy toward anyone who enters the Valley. Then my next question is, did you leave the Valley of your own volition, or did someone force you out?"

"Neither, exactly. Scott brought me out." Briefly, I wondered why I hadn't seen his gloating face at school this morning.

"Who?"

"Scott, we go to school with him. I'm surprised Gem never mentioned him, half the year's in love with him. Anyway, he was in the Valley, and he found me, or I found him, I can't remember exactly. It's all a bit confusing." I frowned again and rubbed my forehead, cursing my fragmented memory. "He said the Valley had lulled me to sleep, and then... he used death magic to bring me home." I hesitated for a second, then my fears came tumbling out. "That's okay, isn't it? I mean, that *I* didn't use it. I did *want* to leave, but I didn't use the magic myself. So I won't be corrupted by the Valley, will I?"

Mrs Caro sighed and leaned back against the seat, eyes closed. "I don't think so."

"Can... can I rescue Gem now?" I ventured after a moment.

Mrs Caro laughed hollowly. "You'll have to."

My fingers twisted in my school skirt. "What do you mean?"

"Edge—do you mind me calling you that? It's how Gemma refers to you."

I nodded.

"Edge, the Valley is a dangerous place." She rubbed her cheek. "You already know that it's the land of death, while Sanctuary is the land of life, and to travel to either you need to use the power of death or life respectively."

I nodded again, wondering where she was going.

"What they don't tell you is this: life and death exist in a precarious balance in the middle worlds. But wait, before I get to that, you know about them being multidimensional, yes?"

"There can be thousands of people there at once but we can never see them," I said, reciting what Quoise had told me. How was this relevant? I crinkled my brow. "And they're all connected like crinkled paper?"

"You've been talking to Gem." Mrs Caro smiled tightly. "But yes, that's right. You can't see them."

I inhaled as I realised what that meant. "I can't find Gemma."

Mrs Caro softened. "You can see people who entered at the same point that you did. If you travelled over at the same place, your chances of seeing her would be vastly improved. But we don't want you to use death magic, and it doesn't matter anyway, because you have another advantage. You're a Road Master. And because you're a Road Master, it doesn't matter if you entered at a different point, on a different dimension; you can use your magic to find her."

"I tried that last time." I bit my lip and stared out the window. The rain made the green of the grass and leaves bright and it reminded me of the unreal colours of the Valley. "I fell asleep."

"Death magic is powerful," Mrs Caro said. "It's not like life magic, quick and spontaneous and creative; it's slower, more ponderous, erosive. Because of that, people underestimate it—but slow doesn't mean less powerful."

"Like water," I murmured, watching as rivulets formed on the roadside, washing through the dirt.

"Yes, like water. And the Valley is the accumulation of death magic; the land is slow and quiet, but strong. Convincing. And it recognises power—as does Sanctuary."

"What do you mean?" I asked, turning back to her. "How can land recognise anything?"

"Not the land." She shook her head. "The power feeding it. It senses power in the visitor and responds accordingly. Sanctuary, for example, will be more real, more beautiful, depending on your personal ability. For the weakest, it's nothing but a hazy, shimmering dream that leaves a lingering feeling of satisfaction."

I thought of Gem and I, running through Sanctuary with the wind in our hair, patting the foals, listening to the shush of the ocean. "You mean... I'm powerful?" A thrill ran through me, and for the first time in days, it wasn't a bad one.

Mrs Caro smiled. "Yes, Edge. You and Gemma are quite powerful. But right now, the important thing is that you are the right *amount* of powerful."

"What do you mean?"

"The last thing I need to tell you is the most important. I said before that life and death exist in a precarious balance in the worlds between worlds."

I swallowed, not knowing where she was going, but knowing from her tone that I wasn't going to like what she had to say.

"Both Sanctuary and the Valley feed off the power of their visitors, Edge. Usually, it doesn't matter who comes and goes. But something in the Valley isn't right. Gemma told me that you discovered that's where the shadows are spawning."

Fear curled up in my chest, cold and heavy. "It's leaking," I whispered, remembering first Gemma's words, then Scott's. "The shadows are spreading."

Mrs Caro nodded. "They're leaking. At all the entry points to the Valley, across all the worlds, the shadows are oozing out, and things are getting sucked across." Her voice trembled and she took a deep breath. "I did some poking around. Gemma is the first *person* to be taken. It's only been things until now."

My hands fisted as I thought of my pen with its lingering sense of the Valley all over it. Had Scott been telling the truth? "I still don't see how this relates to me," I said, throat dry.

Mrs Caro sighed. "I know. It's a lot to explain. I'm sorry. Basically, Mr Caro and I and a couple of others we know—who are very smart, but not very powerful—anyway, with the Valley leaking all over the place we suspect that there's a power imbalance there somehow. It's too strong, stronger than it should be, so we can't risk sending anyone too powerful over there in case they succumb and the Valley gains *their* power.

"But I can't just ask anyone to go into the Valley either," she continued. "Because you have to be powerful enough to see the Valley fully formed to have a chance of finding her. The Road Mastery counts for a lot, of course," she added. "How strong *is* your Road Mastery?"

I leaned over, head in hands. "Strong." *Frogs*, I thought. *Froggity, froggity, frogs.* This was Not Good, with a capital Not, and a capital Good. "I have the right amount of power," I mumbled into my palms.

"You have the right amount of power. You can actually see and feel and interact with the Valley, but you're not so strong that your presence there will immediately tip the balance in its favour. And with your Road Mastery, you have a chance of actually tracking Gemma down."

I can't go.

I have to go.

I don't want to go.

I have to rescue Gemma.

And Veve.

I twitched my fingers, imagining Veve's soft fur. I sat up. "I have to go."

"No. You don't have to," Mrs Caro said quietly.

I looked at her. Her eyes were wide and shining, her lips pressed tightly together and her hands gripping her thighs. "If I don't go?"

Mrs Caro swallowed. "Then I'll go. And we'll hope and pray that I can somehow track her down before the shadows find me, and if not that I can find a way to die if the shadows get me, because that would be better than the alternative."

I laughed hollowly, shook my head and popped the door. "I'll go," I said. I climbed out into the rain and stood there as it plastered my hair to my face.

Mrs Caro came around and stood beside me, her arm around my shoulders. "The Valley isn't fussy, Edge. It'll take any power it can get. It will try to seduce you, cloud your mind, make you think it's a wonderful place. It wants all the power it can get."

I fought back a scream, remembering my brain fog, the way I'd slowed in my search and eventually stopped, forgetting completely what I'd been there for. And those words it had whispered, like a caress as I'd fallen asleep: Welcome home.

A home was what I wanted more than anything in the world, a home where I belonged and was safe. What if it happened again? What if I wasn't strong enough to resist the Valley this time? And what if I *was* strong enough to give it enough power to tip the balance?

"What will happen if the Valley gets too powerful?" Rain dripped from the tip of my nose.

"The shadows will leak out everywhere, I expect," Mrs Caro said. "After that, I've no idea."

I weighed up my options. On the left, try to save Gem and Veve and risk the entire universe, because no one actually *knew* that I wasn't powerful enough to tip the balance, or that I *was* powerful enough to find them while resisting the Valley. On the right, stay here, be safe (at least until the shadows devoured the world), but risk the lives of my best friend and the puppy I'd helped raise.

Search for Gem, maybe fail, destroy the world.

Sit back, do nothing, fail my friend, and probably watch the shadows devour the earth.

Such. Great. Options.

"You do have one advantage," Mrs Caro said.

"What's that?"

"You have the unicorn ward."

I glanced down at the bump under my sock. "It's a ward?"

Mrs Caro nodded. "Unicorns are the only creatures who belong equally to life and death, as I'm sure the fairies told you—though maybe not. I'm still surprised Quoise gave you the ward at all," she said, frowning.

Guilt plucked at my stomach. "Well, Quoise did say not to tell anyone."

"Mm. Still. Anyway." Mrs Caro refocused. "At least you can walk freely into the Valley."

"At least?" I snorted, thinking I'd much rather the ward did something truly fantastic, like rescue Gem so I didn't have to go into the Valley at all.

"Yes." Mrs Caro held me at arm's length and searched my face. "Because otherwise, the only way into the Valley would be death magic. Thank heavens for small mercies," she added as she drew me into a wet, crushing hug.

I hugged her so hard my arms hurt. I loved Gem and Veve—but the thought of using death magic filled me with dread. "Thank heavens for small mercies," I whispered, and cried.

17

I STOOD IN the clearing, glaringly aware of my skin. Never before had it seemed so fragile—too fragile to protect against the rain dribbling down through the trees, let alone the power of the Valley and its shadows.

Mrs Caro laid a hand on my shoulder. "You can do this, Emma. I believe in you. And I know Gemma does too."

I'm sure it was fantastic to have so many people believing in me, but right then the person I needed to believe in me most was *me*, and I was having a hard time doing it.

Mrs Caro took a deep, focused breath. "Just remember to focus on the ward. And don't accept anything anyone offers. Even..." Her grip tightened. "Even Gemma, until we get her out of there and make sure."

I nodded, squeezing my forehead and hoping that all my newfound knowledge wouldn't leak out my ears.

"Off you go then." Mrs Caro released me and stepped back.

I dug around in my pocket for a seed and crouched. In some ways, it would have been a lot simpler if I'd just been able to travel straight into the Valley—but no way was I going to use death magic to get there. So, Sanctuary it was. I'd have to walk the long way—and convince the fairies to let me through again.

"Here goes nothing," I muttered as I thrust the seed into the soil. Nerves thrummed like electricity.

"Remember, I'll meet you at the Lodge at four," Mrs Caro said. "Find her, Edge."

Fear rippled through me as I slid toward Sanctuary, but just as suddenly warmth overtook it and I was there.

Sanctuary. A place of safety. I remembered asking Quoise if it was safe the first day I'd visited. It felt like a lifetime ago, though it was barely over a week. It hurt that it hadn't turned out to be a refuge after all.

Not that it was Sanctuary's fault, I thought as I left the alcove. Stupid Valley. Stupid shadows. I rubbed the goosebumps from my arms and set off. The breeze brought with it the smell of salt water, and I wondered if I wished hard enough whether I could just turn into a dolphin and swim away. Sanctuary was magic, right? Surely it could turn me into a dolphin if I wanted, and then I'd never have to worry about anything ever again.

Unless shadows liked water too. Ha.

I neared the stables and something hissed. Pushing wet hair back off my face, I peered around and realised it was—for reasons best known only to her—Quoise, beckoning me behind the building.

I followed, impatient. "What is it?"

She trembled in mid-air. "You're back. Are you... Are you okay?"

"I'm fine," I said, biting off the words. "What do you want?"

"You... You couldn't find Gemma?"

I shook my head. "But I'm going back again and this time I will find her, and you can't stop me."

Quoise bit her lip. "Edge, it's been over twelve hours. The chances of finding her—"

"Aren't great, I know. Mrs Caro brought me." I lifted my hand to Quoise and she landed. "Why are the shadows moving?"

Quoise shook her head. "We don't know."

"So guess."

"It could be any number of things."

"So name a few." I stared her down.

Quoise hung her head. "The balance is out. We don't know how, or why, but there's..." She waved her hands. "A hole, a sinkhole, near the middle of the Valley that's sucking in power." She peeked up at me. "Please don't tell anyone I told you."

"I thought you couldn't travel into the Valley."

"We can't."

"Then how do you know about the sinkhole?"

"All fairies are Road Masters, Edge," she said softly. "Strong ones."

"You can sense the sinkhole from here?" I asked, surprised.

She nodded. "You'll feel it as you get closer, I'm sure of it. You're... you're really serious, aren't you? You're going back in." It wasn't really a question.

"Gemma and Veve are in there," I said, not really answering.

Quoise glanced down and nodded. "At least you're still wearing the ward."

Irritating bloomed. "Quoise, why didn't you tell me about the sinkhole last time? That seems like a useful piece of information to have known. Not to mention the fact that the Valley would try to put me to sleep!"

"I..." She shook her head. "Things have changed since yesterday. The shadows... One of us, one of the fairies..." She hung her head. "Ambergris is gone. *Someone* needs to do something."

She buried her face in her hands. "I'm sorry," she whispered after a long moment. "I didn't want you to get hurt. But no one goes in and out of the Valley, Edge. Not without death."

I wished Quoise was large enough to hug. Instead, I sank to the ground and patted for Quoise to join me. She fluttered down and snuggled by my side. I cupped her with my hand. "I'll be okay," I said to her at last. "Mrs Caro explained to me how to slip between dimensions so I can use my Road Mastery to track Gem down."

Quoise perked up. "Yes, that will make it easier, if you can do it. Do you know what her soulprint looks like?"

Soulprint. So that's what they were called. I shook my head, stomach sinking. "You'd think I would, since I spend all day with her. But I don't know, I guess I haven't figured out how to use my Road Mastery properly yet."

Quoise smiled. "That's something I *can* help you with. I mean, I shouldn't, and *please* don't tell anyone I'm helping you. But if you're certain about going back in again, I have to at least *try* to make sure you survive." She flew into the air. "Come on. Follow me."

She led me up to the Lodge, past the cavernous entry hall with its bustling flocks of fairies, down a glimmering corridor, around a few corners, and into a room whose walls were plated glass. Behind the glass stood row upon row and stack upon stack of tiny, wooden drawers.

Quoise fished out a charm from a chain on her neck, flew midway up the left wall two-thirds of the way along, and pressed the charm against the glass. A portion of it vanished, just enough to allow Quoise to open one of the drawers. "We keep a record of everyone who comes through Sanctuary," she said, extracting a glass vial as long as her leg and bringing it down to me. "Just in case."

I took the vial. "What do I do with it?"

She smiled. "Open the stopper and dip your finger in. Then just use your Road Mastery."

I pulled the cork out of the vial, biting my lip and wondering what to expect. I dipped in a finger; a flash of light consumed my senses. I winced.

"It's all right," Quoise said. "That's just its power activating. You'll see it in a second."

And sure enough, I did. The tube glowed golden through my closed eyelids and I focused on it, opening myself up to my Road Mastery. Quoise sparkled over to my right, a deep iridescent blue the colour of her wings, accompanied by the smell of rain and the soft sound of tinkling bells.

The tube brightened, sucking me into it. A deep, dark blue surrounded me, velvety and soft to the touch, studded with gems that might have been diamonds if they hadn't been twinkling so brightly. Something soft sounded just out of hearing, making the back of my neck itch in irritation—like trying to remember something important I'd just forgotten.

"It's the night sky," I murmured. "Only it's velvet. She's the night sky as a fabric."

Quoise chuckled. "Indeed."

I opened my eyes in wonder. "No wonder she loves glamour." And no wonder she'd irritated me when I'd first met her, I added to myself. That high-pitched noise was fine now I knew what it was, but the constant sensation of being about to remember something would have been a big turn off.

Quoise's chuckle deepened to a laugh as she took the re-stoppered vial and put it away.

"I'd better get going," I said as she returned.

"Wait." She drew a second, smaller vial out from behind her back. She considered it for a long moment, tiny fingertips white with the strength of her grip, then handed it over. "The sinkhole," she whispered.

I took it, heart hammering in my chest, and dipped my pinkie in. Another surge of light, then blackness blacker than black, and the smell of overripe fruit, stagnant water, and fetid carcasses. I gagged.

Quoise took the vial from me and restoppered it. "It shouldn't even *have* a soulprint," she murmured, avoiding eye contact. "I don't know what's wrong."

I wiped my mouth with the back of my hand then rubbed my forehead. "It's awful."

"I know." She returned it to its drawer. "Do you want me to come with you to the border?"

I considered it for a moment, but heading back into the Valley was something I had to do alone, and there was no point pretending otherwise. I shook my head. "I'll be okay. Thank you, though."

She hovered in the air near my face. "I'll keep the other fairies out of the passage again." She placed a hand on my cheek. "Good luck, Emma Tanning. May you do what no one else can."

I bowed my head. "Thank you."

I exited Quoise's passageway and stopped. Goosebumps rose on my arms as I surveyed the border. The shadows had engulfed a tree I was positive had been in Sanctuary the other day. Add that to my list of things to do in the Valley. One: save Gem and Veve. Two: save the world.

Ah ha. Didn't lists make everything look so nice and simple?

Okay, I told myself. *Enough stalling. Butt into gear; let's do this.* I reached down and brushed my fingers against the unicorn ward, making sure it was secure.

I backed up, squared my shoulders, and ran. I jumped over the border, yelling, "Yaaaah! Take that, stupid Valley!"

I landed heavily, rolling my ankle. "Oh joy." I bent down to massage it. "The perfect start to my adventures." I prodded it, trying to determine the extent of the damage. The smell of mint rose up and the ward began to glow, a soft, pale green shot through with gold glitter. Heat seeped downwards toward my damaged ligaments. The light and warmth flared, and the pain was gone.

Heh. Turned out unicorn wards were useful for more than just crossing the border. Nice to have a pleasant surprise for a change. I glanced around me and wondered how many *un*pleasant surprises the Valley held. That put a damper on things.

Better get moving. But which way? I closed my eyes and concentrated on Gem's soulprint, but the woods around me stayed empty. Was I going to have to search every dimension to find her? How long would that take? Mrs Caro had said there was one dimension in the Valley for every entry point, and they knew of at least a hundred of those.

My heart sank as I realised just how impossible finding Gem and Veve was going to be. I closed my eyes again, searching for anything that might give me a starting point.

There, what was that? A patch of darkness darker than the rest, and the smell of rotting fruit. I cracked an eye open to check out my chosen direction. Great. Just perfect. I'd managed to choose the only corridor of swampland in this entire life-forsaken place.

"Oh well," I told myself as I headed off. "It can't be worse than Scott."

18

I TRUDGED THROUGH the swampy muck, reminded of the one and only time Dad had convinced me to go hiking with him. Sure, I had fond memories of the bonding time and all, but I could have lived without a repeat of the mud-in-my-boots, hair, eyes, nostrils, everywhere-else-possible experience.

I tripped and landed face-first. *Eww.* As I pushed myself up, mud dripping off me, I wondered if this was a good time to quit. Home had never seemed so appealing—or so clean.

I ground my teeth. I couldn't turn back now. Gem needed me. I shook off the worst of the mud—and froze.

A hoarse whisper, full of darkness and power, wrapped around me. *"Home. Come to me. So sweet, alive, come home."*

The Valley. Concentrating, I realised that I could sense the whispers with my Road Mastery. I had to wonder if that wasn't the whole reason the Valley seemed to amplify my senses—just so it could hijack them and seduce me. Well. It was *not* going to beat me again. I shut down my Road Mastery to a mere trickle, forcing the whispers from my mind.

I walked. At last I left the swamp behind and headed into more trees, though these ones were mercifully free of yellowed leaves and oozing red sap. Then, just for a change of pace, I walked some more, the ambient heat drying the mud so it caked and chafed.

I still had no clue where I was going, and I had nothing for reference other than the vague sense of shadowy darkness ahead that I checked periodically. My hips ached and sweat was loosening the mud so now it squelched as well as chafed. The air pressure seemed to increase and heat rippled off the ground, the whole world stifling.

Just as I thought I couldn't walk any more, the trees opened up and I saw a shallow valley in front of me—and a dark, shadowy area in the tree line opposite. I sighed, cracked off as much mud as I could, and headed toward it, hoping that this was the right way to find Gem.

Close up, I surveyed the shadows, absently rubbing more dried mud from my arms. Although the shadows seemed scary enough, the power sink still felt distant. I closed my eyes. I was definitely in the right spot; the sinkhole gaped in front of me, a yawning black hole. But somehow, it also *wasn't* there. I needed my Road Mastery to see what was going on, but did I dare risk the whispers?

I cast about, but no other options presented themselves. I sighed and opened my Road Mastery up fully. Hopefully I could find what I needed before the whispers returned.

I frowned. Tiny slices of the sinkhole were less black than the rest—it was layered across the dimensions. I cast up and in, and found what I was looking for: the centre of the power. It was there in front of me, all right—but on a different dimension. If I wanted to get to it, I'd have to figure out how to slip between them.

I opened my eyes and stared. There was no guarantee that this strange power sink had anything to do with Gem and Veve, and they were my first priority. But on the other hand, I didn't have any better clues about their location, and tracking this hole across the dimensions would allow me to figure out how that worked. Mrs Caro had said that Gem was in a different dimension, after all.

I stared at the sinkhole, worrying at my lower lip with my teeth, unable to shake the knowledge that the blackness in front of me contained one heck of a lot of power—enough to allow shadows to spawn and leak through the gaps between worlds.

Gem had been snatched by leaking shadows. The Valley had a soulprint, and it shouldn't. The two facts had to be related.

I sighed, and ran my hand over my head. I'd have to try dimension hopping. Mrs Caro had told me it was a little like travelling to Sanctuary; I had to imagine where I wanted to go and then sort of twist sideways to get there, only instead of just imagining what the new place looked like, I had to use the Road Mastery.

Sometimes physically twisting helped, she'd said, although she'd obviously never done it herself. She couldn't help me any further, saying that I'd just have to use my Road Mastery and hope for the best. I was getting good at hoping for the best.

Using the sinkhole as a focal point seemed to help; where the rest of the landscape around me blurred indistinguishably, I could at least sense the layers of the hole. Maybe that would be enough.

I backed up a few paces and drew up an image of another dimension. The world would look exactly the same as it did now, with all the trees and branches and leaves and even the blades of grass in exactly the same position—but the shadows would be larger, deeper.

When I was confident that the image felt real, I twisted, spinning myself in a tight circle. I felt a flash of nausea, then nothing. Tentatively, I opened my eyes.

The shadows were darker. I grinned. Mrs Caro had warned me that it might not work the first few times I tried it, but I'd done it first go. "Take that, Valley," I said. I closed my eyes briefly to check my position: about halfway closer to the centre of the sinkhole. That was good.

A wave of nausea crashed over me and I groaned. Mrs Caro had also warned that there might be side effects. I wrapped my arms around my stomach and hugged tight, holding my breath against the pain. Who was I kidding? What did it matter if I could skip between the dimensions as fast as blinking? There were still hundreds of them, all as large as the Valley itself, and unless I got some clue about where Gem might be, I'd have to search them all.

Eyes closed against fading nausea, my breath hitched. A flicker of blue in the dimness; a sparkle of diamond and the brush of velvet against my fingertips. Without thinking, I strained toward it and slipped sideways, crossing the dimensions as easily as breathing.

Insubstantial claws shredded against my skin. My eyes flew open and I screamed from the very centre of the Valley's black hole.

19

BLACKNESS RUSHED INWARDS, crushing my mind, my senses, everything. How could I have forgotten how dangerous the Valley was? I cursed myself even as I turned to mush. This was the *last time* the Valley would get the better of me.

Wind rushed and whirled and my head roared. My stomach cramped, nausea rising in waves until I gulped, choked, and threw up. Acid burned my throat and I coughed and gagged, struggling for air.

The shadows pressed against me, cloying my skin, my nostrils, and I couldn't breathe, couldn't see, couldn't think. I whirled, throwing my hands out for something, anything to steady me, but I found only air.

Where were the trees? Had the shadows eaten everything? I thudded to my knees, cradling my head in my hands.

Black. Darkness. Everywhere, in every direction, as far as I could sense—nothing but darkness and thick shadows.

I couldn't even feel the ground; I wasn't falling, but there didn't seem to be anything solid holding me up, either. I caught my breath, heart hammering as I slipped and landed on my butt.

Mrs Caro hadn't mentioned anything like this.

Mrs Caro. Gem. Veve.

Thirty seconds, I told myself. That was how long I had to be scared, and after that, I had to put the fear aside and move. I wrapped my arms around my legs and gasped, fear eating at my chest, hollowing my stomach, and slicking my hands with sweat.

My thirty seconds were up. I inhaled as deeply as I could, sucking in the air and holding it to assure myself that at least, no matter what else happened, I wasn't dead yet. I could still find Gem.

Oh. Gem. Her dark blue soulprint; a patch of shadows lighter than the rest. My heart pounded and hope bubbled up. Gemma had been here. I didn't know Veve's soulprint—I didn't even know if animals *had* soulprints—but hopefully where Gemma had been, Veve had been too. I closed my eyes, squeezing my clammy hands tight, and flung out my Road Mastery.

Nothing.

I sighed and stood up, nausea washing over me for the third time. I froze, unable to convince myself

I wouldn't fall if I tried to move. *Gem*, I reminded myself. *Veve.*

I reached out with my foot and tested the not-ground in front of me. Solid. I could walk. I groaned at the thought of yet another indeterminate hike.

With no landmarks and not even the sense of air on my skin, I had no idea how long I walked, but my legs began to feel heavy and my lower back ached. My left foot had blisters, and its blisters were beginning to get blisters—school shoes are supposed to be sturdy and supportive and all, but they're definitely not designed for hiking. Thankfully, the unicorn ward was more than earning its keep, healing the blisters on my right foot almost as they appeared.

My brain powered down and I drifted into semi-consciousness. It wasn't until I rubbed an itch on my eyelid and saw a faint flicker of light ahead that realised I'd been walking with my eyes closed.

Lacking any better option—I still hadn't seen anything more of Gemma's soulprint—I swung toward the light. It grew brighter, and as I got closer I saw that it was a pillar of charcoal grey and black light, spiralling upwards into nothingness. Despite how bright it seemed, it wasn't strong enough to illuminate anything—that, or there really was nothing here for it to illuminate.

I stumbled to a halt in front of it, shoulders sagging and head pounding.

You are well met, Emma Tanning.

I stared vaguely, sure the voice was a by-product of my exhaustion-addled brain.

Will you speak?

I blinked. "Um, hi?"

The pillar of light sparkled. *Hello.*

"You're... the light, talking?" Well, I was smack in the middle of the Valley, surrounded by unfathomable darkness. I don't know why I hadn't expected weird things.

I am light, and I am power. I am the sum of everything, and what everything might be.

I snorted, fighting the urge to mouth off. I was too tired for this. I had friends to find.

You doubt my nature?

"No," I said. Best not to anger whatever the light actually was. This was the Valley, after all. I bit the inside of my lip. "It's kind of a mouthful, though. Do you have a shorter name?"

Lucky for me, glowing pillars of light didn't seem to understand sarcasm.

Many have called me Master, Emma Tanning.

I raised an eyebrow. "Seriously?" There was no way I was calling anything dead in the heart of the Valley 'Master'. Learned that lesson last time, even if it *had* turned out all right in the end.

I am always serious. The pillar flickered again, showing off. *I am force, I am power, I am inevitable. I am great and vast and wide, and all come to me in the end.*

Yeah, yeah, blah-blah-blah. I twisted around, trying to decide which direction I'd investigate next.

I would that you would come to me, Emma Tanning.

Shivers prickled down my spine. How did the thing know my name, anyway? I shrugged, feigning nonchalance. "I'm here, aren't I?"

It is not quite the same, the light said. *But since you are here, will you come?*

The light sparkled and twinkled, ribbons of black and grey twining and dancing, and I couldn't look away. My thoughts slowed, and I knew I'd been about to say no, but I couldn't quite figure out why. The light was beautiful, and I wanted to go to it, to step into it and embrace it, to let it fill me so I could dance with it too. I stretched out my hand.

Will you come?

"I... don't know." I'd meant to say no, really I had... But something about the voice seemed familiar, and it half seemed to me that this voice had spoken to me once of home, of freedom.

The light flared. *Yes,* it said. *Home. This is my offer to you, if you will come: all the power of the universe at your command. The power over life and death, the power to keep any creature from dying. The power to create something out of nothing, to live forever and ever, to rule the world as you see fit and to sculpt it into something better and more perfect, something truly yours.*

But more than that, Emma Tanning: think what you could do with such power.

Images flashed into the air in front of me, breathtaking in their clarity. Me, laughing with Gemma and Grace, surrounded by all my old friends. My old room, comfy pillows softer and more inviting than ever. Anna, smiling and laughing, arms wrapped around Kade's waist. Mum and Dad, happy and peaceful, not even a hint of danger in the air.

My breath hitched in my throat and an intense homesickness hit me right in the gut. Why couldn't I ever seem to stop running? Why couldn't I just find a home that would be safe? First Melbourne had been stripped away from us, and now Sanctuary was being taken too.

Safe. With all the power in the world, I could make a new home, and this time I make sure that no one would ever take it from me again. My family, my friends—we'd all be safe, forever.

Do you accept my offer? the light said, reaching out to caress me.

I stiffened, closing my eyes. It was evil. It had to be. This was the Valley.

But I wanted the safety the vision had offered me so much. It wasn't wrong to want to be safe, was it?

"Ye—" My ankle itched and I frowned at it. The ward. I scratched and as I did the smell of mint filled the air. Another light appeared, this one pale green, much fainter than the grey-and-black pillar and far less impressive.

Edge, said the new light in a voice that tickled my subconscious. I'd heard this voice before too, though I couldn't place where. My frown deepened. Had it once led me to safety?

Edge, can you hear me?

"I can."

The pillar of light flashed and I cringed away, shielding my eyes. *Speak not to others in my presence!* the light cried. *I am your master now!*

I inhaled deeply, mint filling my awareness and driving away the fog that I hadn't noticed clouding my thoughts. "No," I said, squaring my shoulders. "You're not my master."

You said yes. That is enough.

My stomach clenched. "No, I only said 'ye'. That's not yes."

She is right, the mint voice chimed in. *You have no claim on her.*

That is for her to decide, the pillar snapped. *Emma Tanning, do you accept my offer or do you not?*

Images flared to life around me again, bigger and brighter and stronger. I cried out as their reality overwhelmed me. My path was suddenly so clear: let go, just release my fears and worries and I could step right in to this heaven and it would be real, and true, and mine forever and ever.

I stepped forward.

Green light flickered in my parents' eyes.

My chest tightened and I reached out to them.

"No," I whispered. "Please."

Cracks rippled over their skin and a minty breeze breathed in my face. *It is not real.*

I grabbed at the fragments of the images, trying desperately to hold them together, but the hairline fractures became chipped edges became chasms and the false people exploded outwards, shards of skin vanishing into the dark. "No," I sobbed. "No, please! Let it be real!"

It can never be real. It is a lie.

My chest ached, but even as I clutched at the shattered fragments of my dream life, I recognised the truth the minty voice spoke. This *wasn't* my life, it wasn't real—and any power that could make it real could only ever create an illusion. A mask on a corpse.

With tears streaming down my cheeks, I opened my hands and watched as the last of the ragged pieces fluttered away.

The pillar of light flared. *No! You will be mine!*

I screamed as fingers of light stabbed at me. "No!" I shouted. "I won't, I won't!"

The green light flared also. *Leave her be*, it said, and the black-and-grey pillar froze, shrieking. The green light inched toward it and as they met, light exploded. Screeches battered my ears and I clapped my hands over my ears.

20

WHEN THE NOISE stopped, I lifted my head to see—nothing. I was alone again, and there was nothing to do but walk.

The blackness weighed me down. Maybe I'd just been imagining things like trees, and grass, and light. Maybe I'd always been stuck in this soul-sucking darkness, and I'd simply invented other worlds for entertainment. I stopped. Was there any point continuing? Even if I *was* looking for someone called Gemma, even if she *did* exist, how was trawling through this indeterminate nothingness going to help?

A smudge of light ahead and to the right interrupted my thoughts. I swung around toward it. Someone was standing in the middle of the light, a boy with blond hair and—I looked down at my own clothes. They were hard to recognise through the dirt caked over them, but I thought perhaps that the boy's uniform matched mine.

He turned toward me and I had a flash of recognition. "Scott!"

Good. I hadn't imagined my other world after all.

"What are *you* doing here?" he said, shocked. He furrowed his brow and scowled at me. "I thought I made myself clear: *Stay. Away!* Or are you just going to haunt me forever?"

"I'm not haunting anything," I snapped. "I'm trying to find..." I hesitated, wondering if I should tell him about Gemma. "Something," I said instead.

He raised an eyebrow and looked pointedly at the darkness. "Here?"

I balled my hands into fists by my sides and lifted my chin. "This is where I saw it last." Close enough to true; I'd seen Gemma's soulprint at the edge of the shadows.

Scott's eyebrows shot up. "In the heart of the Valley?"

I squirmed. I knew this was the sinkhole, the part of the Valley that was sucking power in, but hearing Scott say it made it uncomfortably real.

Scott laughed. "You didn't realise? You walked right on in here and you didn't even realise what it was? Princess, you're so stupid you don't even know how much you don't know."

"Oh yeah?" I said, temper flaring beyond rational thought. I stepped forward. I'd had enough of all this. I ached, my head pounded, I was bone-tired and I just wanted to find Gemma and go home. "Well what are *you* doing here? Enjoying a little casual murder, Scott?"

"What did you say?" His voice was eerily calm as he matched me step for step.

"You think you're so big and powerful," I said, squeezing my nails into my palms so I wouldn't hit him. "But you're using the power of *death*, Scott. *Death*. At least what I know, I know about life."

"Sanctuary?" he sneered. "That's what you're comparing this to?" He laughed. "Sanctuary doesn't have *half* the power of the Valley, Princess. You can do things here that you couldn't even *imagine* in Sanctuary."

My stomach twisted as I realised he was probably right. "But what will you have in the end, Scott?" I said quietly, glimpsing a future devoured by the shadows. "What will be left when the Valley has it all?"

"Left? Left?" Scott laughed again. "Princess, what's *left* won't matter. Because what I will have in the end is everything." A wistful expression crossed his face, and I wondered what images the pillar of light had offered him. "Death comes for us all," he said, also quiet now. "You can't win by avoiding it."

Tears prickled my eyes. "Oh, Scott. Is that what you really believe?" I asked, overcome by pity now I saw what his exterior hid: a desperate little boy.

His face hardened. "I don't *believe*, Princess," he spat. "It's true. Embrace the power of death, and live forever." He drew something out of his pocket.

I tensed, expecting perhaps another nearly-dead mouse—and my breath caught in wonder. Sitting on his outstretched palm was a fairy, a perfect sepia replica of Quoise or Ruby or any of the others. But instead of eyes, lifeless glass gave her a glazed appearance, and as she shifted I noted a tiny key sticking out of her back. "Clockwork," I breathed.

Scott stared at her. "No," he said. "So much more." He tossed his hand upwards and I tensed, ready for the fairy to fall and smash. But instead, she shot up into the air, wings fluttering frantically until she righted herself and hovered over Scott's shoulder. He smiled—and I shied away. Hunger lit up his eyes and touched his lips; his smile was mirthless and cruel.

All of a sudden I noticed what I'd been seeing with my Road Mastery all along. Scott's soulprint was black, I'd known that, but standing here in the darkness I realised something else: his soulprint wasn't just a smudge of black in the dark. It *was* the dark. His soulprint blended seamlessly with the heart of the Valley, and I couldn't find where one ended and the other began.

The Valley didn't need me. It had Scott, and he had darkness enough to feed the Valley until it grew to consume the entire world. I stepped backwards.

Scott's lips stretched wider. "You see, then," he said. "It's not really death magic. It's just... rearranging life." Abruptly he raised his fist in the air and the fairy launched toward me on a wave of Scott's power. She pulled her lips back in a snarl, revealing vicious, pointed teeth.

I shouted and scrambled backwards, losing my footing. The fairy tucked her wings back and dove. The invisible floor sagged beneath me. My heart lurched and something snapped, cracked, and I fell.

Twist! I screamed at myself as I plummeted through a world made of ink, pursued by Scott's awful parody of life. *Twist!*

I threw myself sideways in the air, but I couldn't clear my mind enough to imagine another place. *Any place*, I told myself. *Anywhere!* But the only thing I could think of was a stretch of velvet night, studded with diamond stars. The fairy scratched at my arm, tiny slices that stung like acid.

Frantic, I twisted again—and the buzz of the fairy stopped. A heartbeat later, I slammed into the ground. My breath left me in a whoosh and I lay gasping and gaping, not even enough air to cry.

21

GRADUALLY MY HEART rate slowed and I found enough oxygen to breathe. The realisation that Scott was fuelling the shadows kept my head reeling, though. What could I do about it? I had to do *something* about it; I couldn't just leave Scott to his own devices in there with his mad, reanimated fairies and overwhelming shadow-soulprint, not if I wanted a chance of getting rid of the shadows. But Gem and Veve needed me more. I pushed myself upright, groaning at my host of new bruises. First things first. Save Gem and Veve, then worry about the fate of the world.

I stood up, dusted myself off stiffly, and stared around. Shadows licked at nearby tree trunks. I was already backing away before I realised that they washed up against the bright edge of my clearing as though there was a physical barrier.

I sagged in relief, thinking that for now, I couldn't possibly get any luckier.

Then I heard the barking.

Spinning around, I stood stunned for a moment as Veve and Gem made their way across the clearing toward me, Veve leaping forward in great bounds before realising Gem had fallen behind and racing back to round her up. Something tickled my cheek, and I realised it was tears.

Then, gasping, I was running toward them, my eyes blurry, my chest tight, but my shoulders suddenly lighter than they'd been in weeks. Veve bounced up against me, toenails scraping my legs, but I didn't care, because she was there, and so was Gem. I drew Gem into the tightest hug in the world, and she squished me back, and just for a second, everything was right.

I held her at arm's length and scrutinised every inch of her, and my stomach sank. "Are you okay?" I said, and she nodded, but wouldn't meet my eye. "What... What happened?"

She gave a half-hearted smile and shrugged. "It doesn't matter, does it? You found us." She gave me the barest flicker of a glance. "How?"

"Your soulprint," I said. "I found it right when I needed to."

No response. I bit my lip.

But before I could question her further, white and gold flashed in the light, and it smelled like I'd crushed an entire potful of mint under my feet. For the first time in weeks, maybe months, my chest wasn't tight.

"Look," I whispered, spinning Gem around.

"I know," she whispered back. "She's been looking after me."

I stood transfixed as the unicorn made her way over to us, and as she walked, my entire world was caught up in white so pale it made paper dark, gold so bright it dimmed the sun, and the faintest traces of pale green in her mane and tail that reminded me of sea foam.

At last, she stopped in front of us and dipped her head. I bobbed the most awkward curtsey in existence. "Hello," I offered.

"Well met," the unicorn replied. "You have come to take them home?"

I opened my mouth, then changed what I was going to say. "Are *you* coming home?"

Something in the unicorn's face changed—her eyes a little tighter, perhaps—as she answered, "I am bound to this place a little while longer. The balance must be kept. I thank you for pulling me out of the darkness of the Valley, but if I leave now, night will fall. You must restore the balance. But first you must take Gemma home." She turned her head to the side, gaze boring into me.

I swallowed, not sure what she was asking. It was Scott and his stupid experimenting that had put the balance out, not me. How was *I* supposed to restore it if even she couldn't?

"Alas," the unicorn continued, "I cannot come with you, but I can take you some of the way. Will you ride?"

My eyes widened. "Ride?" I breathed.

The unicorn tossed her mane. "I am more than capable of carrying you both," she said haughtily.

Gem giggled and I cut her a sharp look. "Of course you are," I said. "I just..." I floundered for a moment before regaining myself. "We would be honoured." This time I made a slight bow, and although it was hardly the most natural thing I'd ever done, it was a whole lot less awkward than the curtsey. Either way, the unicorn seemed happy with it, and turned broadside on so we could mount up.

"Um," I said, pausing with one fist wound in her mane and the other hand atop her back. "What... What should I call you?" It felt weird to be simply climbing on board a unicorn, and outright rude to do so without at least introducing myself.

"Sorry," Gem said, wincing and seeming for a moment more like her usual self. "Edge, this is Aphros, Sanctuary's unicorn. Aphros, Edge."

"Hi, Aphros," I said as Gem gave me a boost up.

"Hold tight now," Aphros said, and I just had time to wrap both hands in her mane and feel Gem's arms grip around me when she launched away like a rocket.

Before we knew it, we'd come to the base of the immense mountain and Aphros halted. "I am sorry," she said, flicking her tail. "This is as far as I may go."

We dismounted, Veve gambolling around at our feet. As Gem stepped away, I hesitated. "Please," I said. "What do you mean that the balance is out? Can I fix it?"

Aphros bumped her nose into my hand, and the darkness behind my eyes exploded into light.

Well, not all of it was light; it was a great, seething mass, bright golden light intertwined with darkness, shifting—alive. But one thing was clear: the darkness was winning.

"This is the balance," she said softly.

I nodded, lip between my teeth.

"That is why I cannot leave," she said, so soft it was hard to hear her over the crush of leaves as Veve and Gem moved. "Were I to leave this place, darkness would be free to rule. And from here, it could touch all the worlds."

I shuddered, thinking of the horrible bushes back home. "What can I do?"

"Restore the balance."

"But *how*?"

"The boy has given the Valley's power life. You must stop him. If you do not, the Valley will extract all of his life force for its own—it will be free to roam the worlds, and the boy will be dead."

I shuddered. Great. All I had to do to save the world was stop Scott. Good thing it wasn't anything too difficult.

Sweat beaded on my forehead and ran down my temples. My shirt clung to me, and I thought I might finally understand how it felt to be a fish, constantly breathing water.

Ahead, Gem slumped against a tree and groaned. "Why does it have to be so *hot?*"

I wiped the sweat from my upper lip and nodded, leaning over and resting on my knees. Beside me, Veve panted heavily, sides heaving, her tongue slopping thick, gooey saliva all over the ground. "Poor beast," I said, half-heartedly ruffling her ear.

In response, she flopped to the ground in the shade. I was so tempted to join her.

Gem bolted upright.

"What? What is it?"

Her face had gone deathly pale, and her hands fisted in the hem of her shirt. "The shadows," she said. "The shadows moved."

My stomach dropped and I stared wildly. "Where? Which ones?"

She pointed ahead, directly between us and Sanctuary. I concentrated on them, willing them to stay still just long enough for us to get home.

Nothing moved. I shook my head. "Gem, I think you're imagining things. The shadows before didn't stop and start, they just came after me. And they whispered. These shadows are quiet." I took her by the arm. "Come on. It'll be okay."

Gem yanked her arm back. "I am not going into the shadows."

I frowned at her. "Gem, these are just normal shadows, I promise. They're not going to hurt you. I should know."

"No!" Her voice was tight with barely-submerged panic. "You can't make me!"

"Gem, this is the way home. There are shadows everywhere right now," I said, gesturing to the forest around us, "and it's getting late. Which means soon there will be more shadows, and we won't be able to tell the real ones from the dangerous ones."

As if on cue, Veve leapt to her feet and barked, tail straight and stiff, the corners of her mouth and ears drawn forward.

"I can't go in there," Gem said, backing away. "I won't."

I shoved aside my own rising panic. I had to focus on getting Gem home. "Gem," I said, taking her arm gently. "The shadows in front of us are normal ones, I promise. This is the way home. It's going to be fine."

Her eyes showed far too much white and her breath came in ragged jerks, but she allowed me to pull her forward a step.

Veve growled. I turned my head just slightly, not wanting to panic Gem any further. My heart leapt. Shadows, Valley ones this time, moving slowly through the trees behind us.

"Gemma," I said in my best no-nonsense voice, "it's time to go. You mother is waiting for you, and for me, and I am taking you back there alive and unharmed. *Let's go*."

She took another step, breath hitching, then another, until she stopped on the fringe of the shade under the trees.

"Come on," I said, ignoring Veve growling behind us and the flickering of black in the edges of my vision. "In we go." I stepped forward, expecting Gem to come with me, but instead she jerked back on my arm, her breaths getting faster and faster.

"I can't do it Edge, I can't, I'm sorry, I can't," she babbled. "He'll see me, he'll find me, he'll get me for sure. I can't go in there. I can't."

"Who?" I frowned. "Scott?"

"No, *not* Scott!" she said, voice high pitched and squeaky. "*Him*! Because he was there, in the dark, and I was lost and alone and I had no idea what had happened or where I was, and he said he'd help me, he did." Tears spilled down her cheeks and her fingers knotted in the hem of her shirt. "And the light, it was so beautiful." She gulped, and nerves zinged down my limbs and into my fingers and toes.

"Gemma," I said, very quietly, with absolute control, watching as the shadows crept into the light behind us. "Did you agree to his bargain?"

She sobbed.

"Gemma," I said more forcefully. *"Did you agree?"*

"Yes."

I reeled like I'd been punched into the ocean, and there were no words I could find to drag me back to the surface. A bubble of anger rose, and I clung to it like a life raft until I could see Gemma sobbing in front of me again. "How could you?" I whispered— but I knew how. I'd so very nearly done the same thing, and I wasn't really angry at Gem, but at myself for nearly being caught by the shadows.

Shadows.

Veve wasn't barking.

I turned slowly, fear a molten ball in my stomach. Veve stood frozen, ringed by shadows that shifted and melted a foot away from her. Her eyes rolled as she tried to keep them in sight, but she seemed to know that she shouldn't move. "You'll have to jump," I said quietly. "Come on, girl. Jump over this way."

Gem turned beside me and inhaled sharply. "Veve!"

If she hadn't stopped to panic, Veve might not be trapped right now; but on the other hand it was nice to know that she cared about my dog. And seeing Veve stuck seemed to galvanise her; she straightened her shoulders and frowned in her classic thinking face. "We have to distract them so Veve can jump out," she said.

My heart pounded. Distract them. I knew what she meant, of course: one of us needed to touch the shadows, draw them away. And Gemma had said yes to the Valley.

"I'll go," she said, jaw set. "The Valley's already got me anyway, so it shouldn't want to hurt me."

"Don't be ridiculous." I pushed her gently out of the way. "I've beaten them before, I can do it again. Also," I said, indicating the unicorn hair ward. I gave a stretched smile. "I'll be fine."

I edged toward the shadows. "As soon as I touch them, reach over and grab Veve's collar," I said. "Then run like the blazes. Sanctuary's that way."

"I know where Sanctuary is," Gemma said, and her eyes sparkled with unshed tears. "Thank you."

"Heh," I said. "Don't thank me. There are still the zombie trees to fight through."

Half a smile. "It's going to be okay."

She *had* to say that. My control slipped a little, and I took a deep breath. "Sure. Ready?"

She nodded.

I stepped to the edge of the shadows and fighting against all my instincts, dipped my toes in. Cold dread washed over me.

"So sweet, so sweet your life."

I pulled back, but the shadows followed, swirling and massing. Out of the corner of my eye I saw Gemma snatch at Veve and dash back.

"We're clear!" she said. "Veve's okay."

The shadows wound around my ankle. *"Hold you, touch you, so warm, so alive."*

I tried to kick free, but they clung tighter, inching their way toward my knee. I fought down the panic that threatened to suffocate me. "I'm stuck," I shouted. "Just take Veve and go!"

"No! I'm not leaving you here!"

"Want your life, so sweet."

I twisted around and glared as Gem set Veve down and ran toward me. "Go away! I'll be fine!"

Veve barked ferociously.

"...sweet, welcome home..."

"No." Gem caught my arm and pulled.

I slipped and fell. Shadows leapt up to my waist and spread down my other leg.

"Home, coming home, coming to us, touching us, life, we want your life."

Gem heaved again, but the shadows stretched with me, only a few strands snapping back like over-taxed rubber bands.

"Come, come home."

Cold.

Everything from my waist down was cold, and it was slowly rising, like stepping into a pool in the middle of summer—only this time I knew there'd be no resurfacing.

"...*want your life, life so sweet...*"

"Emma, your ankle!" Gem shouted.

I looked down. The unicorn ward! Around it, my ankle was free of shadows. Tears sprang up. "I don't know what to do!"

"*I* don't know!" Gem said, still holding me tightly under my arms. "But if you could get the ward to cover all of you..." She pressed her forehead against mine, upside-down, and it was sweaty and cool. "Please don't die."

The shadows climbed. "*Liiiife. So sweet... Come home, sweet home, sweet life.*"

The cold made it hard to breathe; I took short, shallow gasps. How on earth was I supposed to extend the ward? I closed my eyes, fighting to clear my mind—and saw the minty-green wreath around my ankle. The unicorn's soulprint. That's how it protected against the shadows.

Instinctively I reached out to the ward's glow, both with my mind and my fingers.

"What are you doing?" Gemma shrieked, but even as the shadows closed around my hand, I shook my head. This was the only way.

"*Home! Come home, come life!*"

The shadows, sensing victory, leapt up my arm.

Gem sprang away. Good. I couldn't rescue both of us.

I touched the ward, and in my mind's eye I saw a flash of silver. I got a strange sense of being outside my own body and caught glimpses of silver and lace, and the soft smell of old, faded roses. Nausea welled in my gut, like I'd just seen my own insides plastered on the ground.

I forced myself to concentrate. With my fingers as the bridge, I trickled some of my own soulprint out to meet the greenness of the ward. Another flash of silver lit up the space behind my eyes and the greenness billowed and blossomed.

The shadows screeched, a noise almost too high to be heard that made all my hair stand on end. I fed a little more of my soulprint into the unicorn ward, and the green bloomed out around me. The shadows shrieked and jerked back as though stung.

I lay still for a moment, panting and wide-eyed as I waited for the writhing shadows to grab me again.

Gem snatched at me from behind and dragged me to my feet. "Come on!" she said. "Run!"

We took off through the trees. I stumbled and slid, but Gem hauled me upright. Veve bounded along in front. The trees roared as we ran under them. They grabbed at us, branches tangling in our hair, our clothes. Scratches stung my skin and my chest burned from the cold of the shadows; panic chased us like a sheepdog, nipping at our heels.

Veve yelped and fell. Gem jerked away and back again in an instant, Veve's collar firmly in her grip.

Trees whipped and slashed. Blood ran into my eye from a cut on my forehead; soon I'd have no skin left. I'd fall to the ground any second and not be able to get up, and the shadows would find me there and devour me.

Veve yipped and rocketed out of Gemma's grip. Gasping, I lifted my head and saw green.

The border.

I stumbled; Gem righted me. She tripped; I caught her. Together, lungs burning and hearts exploding, we pounded toward the greenery.

Clean air fizzled over us. Branches no longer reached for us; twigs didn't catch in our skin and clothes. We looked at each other, gasping. Something burned my ankle and I jumped. The ward. I reached to touch it and it crumbled to ash, leaving behind the acrid smell of burning mint. "We made it," I said and sank to the ground.

Gemma collapsed beside me. "We made it."

22

UNLIKE THE LAST time I fell out of the Valley and back into Sanctuary, no one was waiting to soothe our hurts. Probably, I told myself as we limped toward the passageway, that was a good thing; it certainly seemed like the fairies would be mad if they found out we'd been into the Valley again. Maybe even mad enough to ban us from Sanctuary. But that didn't stop me wishing for something to ease the hundred million pains that had taken up residence in my body.

"I'm sorry," Gem said as we squeezed into the passage, Veve limping along behind.

I hugged her with one arm. "Rubbish. We got out, didn't we? Oops," I added as we half collided. The floor of the passage slopped gently, but it was enough to make us both unsteady.

"Yeah," Gem breathed. "I guess."

I didn't have the energy to reassure her any further. I knew she was probably thinking about that pillar of light—it seemed to lurk in the edges of my vision, reminding me of the life I could have had—but there was nothing we could do about what had happened. I just wished we knew what would happen now that Gem technically belonged to the Valley.

We emerged into the main hall of the lodge, and almost immediately Quoise appeared in front of us.

"You're alive," she whispered, glancing furtively behind her. "Come on, follow me. Quickly."

Gem and I exchanged glances and followed.

Veve whined.

"Aw, come on, girl," I said, summoning up the energy to ruffle her ears. "We're nearly there, I promise."

Quoise led us to a small room with nothing but a couple of couches and another door. "Stay here as long as you need," she said, and began to leave.

"Wait," I said. "The unicorn. Aphros."

Quoise stiffened to attention. "What about her?"

"She's in the Valley," I said. "She helped Gem and Veve."

"Is she trapped?" The sharp concern in Quoise's voice could have sliced steel.

"No." I shook my head. "At least, I don't think so. Not anymore." Visions of tearing green-and-gold away from black during my first visit to the Valley flashed through my head. "But she said that she can't leave, because if she does, the balance will be out, and the Valley will devour Scott and take over the world."

Quoise nodded curtly. "Thank you. Now." She wagged a finger at me. "I don't want you getting it into your head that you need to go running over to deal with that, okay? The fairies can handle it just fine. Just let us do our jobs."

"I promise," I said, not bothering to add that the Valley was the very last place I ever planned on going again.

Quoise left, closing the door behind her, and Gem flopped on the nearest couch. "Scott's involved?" she mumbled into a pillow.

"Yes," I said, heading to the other door. "I'll tell you later. Bathroom!" I exclaimed with delight as I opened the door. "*Shower!*"

"You first," Gem said, arm over her eyes, free hand resting on Veve's head. "I'm just going to lie here for a couple of years."

I flashed a smile and closed myself in the bathroom. I stripped off, turned the water on as hard as it would go, and sighed. It was over.

Well, Captain Moron, Chief Officer of All Things Stupid, Destroyer of My Life *Scott* was still roaming around creating chaos, but still. For *now* it was over. And really, I was done being responsible. For all that Quoise thought she needed to warn us away, I was more than happy to let someone else deal with Scott. I'd only just turned thirteen, for crying out loud. Adults had to be good for *some*thing.

At first the hot water stung my cuts like acid, but I ground my teeth and the pain eased away. I leaned my head against the cool glass and rested.

The water was going cold and my fingers wrinkly by the time I turned the shower off. Voices murmured through the bathroom door—probably Gem and Quoise. I towelled off, then snagged a dry towel from the large stack and wrapped it around me. Hopefully Gem wouldn't kill me for running the water out.

I opened the door, wondering if Quoise would be able to rustle up some clean clothes, and froze. There was a plate half-full of grapes and orange wedges and bread on the table, and Veve was curled up in a tight ball in an arm chair next to a gleamingly-empty silver bowl—but the most startling change to the room was that Mrs Caro sat on one of the couches, Gem snuggled against her side, tear-tracks down both of their faces.

"Um. I'm sorry," I said, and began shutting myself back in the bathroom.

"Edge!" Gem called, right as her mother said, "Emma! Thank you!"

I paused with the door half-closed and leaned against it, not sure if I wanted to go out or stay hidden where I was.

"Em?" Gemma called. "Come on, it's just Mum."

I sighed explosively and went out to perch on the edge of the other couch, clutching my towel. "My clothes are gross," I said by way of explanation.

"It's fine." Mrs Caro gave Gem another squeeze, filthy attire and all.

"Maybe," I agreed. "But only if Mum doesn't kill me for ruining my school uniform." Gem's gaze met mine, and without warning we laughed.

Mrs Caro stared at us for a moment, then joined in. "Oh girls," she said, wiping tears away. "I'm so sorry. And I'm so, so grateful that you made it back alive." She squeezed Gem to her with one arm, and my stomach flip-flopped. When I got home, there would be no celebrations. Well, I'm sure Mum would be pleased Veve was back, but it sucked that I'd just about been to hell and back and couldn't even get a 'well done' from my parents, because they couldn't know about it.

Mrs Caro stood. "Well. I may be a Time Master and all, but if we don't head off very soon, I won't be able to get you back on time, Edge. Gemma," she said, helping Gem up off the couch, "I know you must be desperate to get clean, but can you hold on just until we get home?"

Gem nodded and leaned her head against her mum's shoulder.

"I ran the water out anyway," I confessed.

Gem gave me a mock glare. "Thanks."

Mrs Caro clapped her hands together decisively. "Right then. Edge, there are clean clothes over there. Get dressed and we'll all head home."

Bed, I thought longingly as I scooped up the clothing and headed back into the bathroom. Home.

Mrs Caro dropped me off at half past four, and I went straight to bed. Mum woke me up when she got home and asked if I was okay. I told her I'd gone to sickbay and Mrs Caro had brought me home, since she'd been in at the school anyway.

"Why didn't you call me?" Mum asked.

"Because Mrs Caro was right there," I said. "I promise I'll call you next time, okay?" I squeezed her hand and she squeezed back.

"Okay," she said. "Make sure you do." She fussed, plumping my pillows and smoothing my hair. "Are you going to stay home tomorrow?"

I closed my eyes, imagining how lovely it would be to spend the entire day asleep. I sighed, and shook my head. "No. I have to hand in my art homework."

Mum smiled. "That's very responsible of you."

"You have no idea," I might have said, but she was leaving already and my eyes were closed anyway, and within three seconds I was asleep.

23

I TRUDGED INTO school with two minutes to spare the next morning. Thankfully Mum had offered to give me a lift so I didn't have to get up early for the bus, so I'd managed an even twelve hours of sleep. Shame I still didn't feel much better.

I wondered if Mrs Caro had given Gem a lift this morning, or if battling shadows in fairyland was just par for the course when you were a family of Travellers. I could just imagine the conversation: You fought off soul-sucking shadows? How lovely. Make sure you wash the blood out of your shirt, and don't expect to take a day off school! I snickered as I walked into the building.

"What's so funny, Princess?"

I jumped. For a fraction of a second I hesitated with my lip in my teeth. Then I narrowed my eyes at Scott. "What? No backup this time?"

He lounged against the lockers like he owned the whole freaking world—which, judging by the shadows pooling around his feet, he soon might— and smiled like the cat who got the proverbial cream. "Why? Do I need some?" He quirked an eyebrow at me in a manner that might have been flirty on anyone else.

I ignored him and tried to move past.

Of course, he stepped into my way with his arms folded over his chest. "So. What's so funny?"

I sidestepped him and stalked through the swelling sea of kids, but he trailed behind.

"Finally figured out how pathetic that little play land of yours is?" he jeered. "That what you're laughing at?"

I stopped short and Scott ran into me. Ha. Take that, Mr Smarty Pants. I swivelled to face him. "Number one," I said, counting off on my fingers. "What I find funny is none of your business. Number two, I will never, *ever* stop for you again, understand? And number three, my name is Emma. Not 'the Princess', not 'hey there'; *Emma*. And number four?" I stepped nose to nose with him, grateful not for the first time that I was a little tall for my age. "Never bring your stinking, filthy death magic near me again."

"Oh yeah?" Scott yelled as I spun away. "Well number five: I hate you! I've always hated you, and anyone who says different is a liar!"

I gave him sarcastic jazz hands over my shoulder, then glanced left as Gemma bumped into place. "Hey."

"Hey. What's up?"

"Scott's up. As usual."

She glanced back to where he still stood watching us, and her eyes widened. "Whoa," she said. "He's *hot*."

I raised my eyebrows in the most sceptical face I'd ever had reason to pull. "You're joking, right?"

"No! He totally is!"

I rolled my eyes and dragged her onwards. "I think the Valley addled your brains. Come on." My stomach lurched, but I managed to keep my face blank. If Gem guessed what I was thinking, she'd panic, because what I was thinking was this: She'd agreed to the light's bargain. What if it really *had* messed with her head?

"But seriously!" she said, resisting my efforts to herd her down the hall. "Something about him is different. I... I don't know." She shrugged.

I stopped and took a good long look at Scott, who had finally given up on staring at us and was heading off in the opposite direction. Gemma was right. Something *was* different. Without my Road Mastery, seeing what Gemma would see, he exuded cool confidence. No, not just confidence. Power, raw and effortless. I could see how that might be attractive, especially on someone like Scott, who was admittedly easy on the eyes. But with my Road Mastery open, I could see the truth: the power wasn't his. It was the Valley's. Scott himself was almost gone.

I shook my head. "That's not the kind of gorgeous you want, trust me." This time, Gem let me lead her away.

Roll call passed uneventfully. Science was first up after that, and the class milled around outside, waiting for our pre-test. Most people whispered furiously about possible questions, or muttered parts of the periodic table under their breaths. Even if I hadn't been wound up from spending yesterday in the Valley, the nerves jangling around the hallway would have had me jittering.

I felt like shouting at the class. It was only a pre-test, for crying out loud. It counted for nothing!

By the time Mrs Johnston opened the door, I felt sick. We filtered into the room in silence and took up our usual seats. For me, that meant Gemma on one side and Scott on the other—but for the first time ever, Death-boy didn't even glance at me as he sat down. I was glad, but it still felt weird.

Mrs Johnston told us to open our tests, and I shoved aside thoughts of Scott and Sanctuary and the Valley, and concentrated on the questions in front of me.

As I skimmed the first page, I was immensely grateful that Anna had used me as a revision partner (ha, more like a revision *wall*) for the last few years. This stuff was easy.

Twenty minutes in, Scott raised his hand. Mrs Johnston walked over, and a few seconds later he was scraping his chair back and leaving the room.

I bit my lip. I mean sure, he *might* just have needed the bathroom, but this was Scott we were talking about—and to be honest, right now I wasn't even sure that it *was* Scott. His soulprint was so damaged it could easily be the Valley acting through him instead.

Finish the test, not follow Scott to the Valley, and hope that the fairies caught him before it was too late... Or ditch the test and head back into my worst nightmare on the off chance I could save Scott from the Valley, and the world from Scott?

I heaved a sigh and stuck my hand in the air. Mrs Johnston acknowledged me disapprovingly, but came over. "Yes?"

"May I go to the bathroom?" I whispered in my best 'I'm-so-innocent voice'. "I'm nearly finished."

She glanced at the paper and her eyebrows lifted. "Looks good. Yes, okay, you can go. But be quick. And quiet!"

I snuck out of the classroom and paused in the hallway, closing my eyes to fix on Scott's dark soulprint. Sure enough, he was nowhere near the bathrooms, heading instead to the strip of bush at the back of the school.

I sprinted down the stairs and along the side of the buildings. Whatever else happened, I had to try to stop him crossing; with so much of the Valley's power in him, even that might be enough to drag him under forever. Much as he was an unbearable git, I'd meant what I'd said to Gemma on Monday: no one deserved the shadows. And if Aphros was right, we couldn't afford for the Valley to have him.

Leaving the school buildings behind, I hurried across dry grass to the scruffy gum trees at the back of the school block. White shirt flashed through the trees and I headed toward it.

Scott was concentrating so hard, he didn't even hear me approach; he sat cross-legged in the dirt with his eyes closed, darkness swirling around him. It billowed and spiralled—the Valley was calling to him, or he to it. Either way, the crossing would be over in an instant, and if his soulprint was anything to go by, so would his life.

This was it. I had to stop him.

24

I LAUNCHED INTO a sprint, adrenalin surging. He raised his hands, still oblivious. I slammed into him, wrapping my arms around him and knocking him flat. Sitting on his chest, I did my best to pin his arms the way I'd seen in movies.

Scott lay dazed for a moment, then blinked up at me, slow grin spreading over his face. "Well. This is nice, then."

My impulse was to jerk away, but if I did that he'd be free again. Urgh. I shoved aside my disgust and squeezed his arms tighter. "I thought you hated me now, Mr Smarty Pants."

He sighed, and all of a sudden seemed old. "Emma, let me go."

"No."

He shifted underneath me, ribs rubbing against the insides of my thighs, which catapulted the moment straight to the top of my most awkward moments of my entire life. "You can't stop me, you know," he said, interrupting my conniptions. "Not with this much of the Valley running through me."

I gasped. "You know!"

He frowned. "Of course I know. How would I not know?"

I didn't answer. It was stupid, of course, but a tiny part of me had hoped that maybe it hadn't been his fault, that maybe the Valley had seduced him and taken up residence without his permission. But I'd been into the heart of the Valley, and I'd seen the pillar of light. There couldn't be any doubt: Scott had made a deal with the darkness.

A shout. I swung around to see Gem bursting through the trees. The world pitched sideways, my face slammed into the dirt, and the fetid stink of the Valley overtook my senses.

"Edge!" Gem hauled me to my feet and dusted me off.

"Where's Scott?" I looked around.

"Gone." Gem bit her lip. "Are... are you okay?"

I ground my teeth and bit back a retort. She was only trying to help. "I'm fine. Let me go, I can stand. I'm fine!" I pushed her away and bent double, running my fingers through the grass. Of all the times to have not had my seeds in my pocket.

"Have you got any seeds?" I asked Gem. I froze. No. Seeds would be too slow.

Her face fell. "No. They're in my bag."

I exhaled, straightening casually. "Yeah, mine too. Can you go grab some?"

Gem stiffened, hands fisting at her sides as she scrutinised me. "No," she said at length.

I tried not to let my irritation show. "Please?" With Scott that full of the Valley's power, every split second counted. There was no way I had time to go into Sanctuary and run all the way into the Valley, and I'd be frogged if I'd let Gemma see what I was planning to do next.

After all, it was just death, right? Like the life magic, I guessed there was no minimum threshold for *how much* death. Gemma had said once that you couldn't offer just a little death, but what if you could? I needed her out of the way so I could test out my theory. If it didn't work and we had to go the long way around, we really might as well give up now.

"No." Gem crossed her arms. "Because as soon as I'm out of sight, you're going to try something, and I'm not having you go without me."

"Gemma, just go away," I snapped. Death magic. The very thought of it made me shudder. I *couldn't* let my best friend see me use it.

"Edge." Her voice trembled, though she tried to hide it, and out of the corner of my eye I saw her swipe at her cheeks. "If you tell me again that you don't want me to come with you, then I won't. But I thought we were friends. And friends don't tell each other to get out when they need help most."

My chest ached. She had no idea what she was asking. I shook my head and raised the other thing worrying me instead. "You agreed to the Valley's bargain, Gemma. Have you stopped to think that maybe, just maybe, that's how Scott got into this whole mess in the first place? That maybe, now that the Valley has him, it will want you too?"

She grabbed me by the shoulders. "But don't you see? That's *why* I have to come. It will think I'm coming back to it, and it will *help me*. Otherwise how would it ever be able to get ahold of me, if it killed me as soon as I went back? It... It would be like a virus that was too strong and killed its host before it could infect a new one and then died too." She looked proud and defiant at that.

I hesitated. Surely Scott hadn't been corrupted in just two short visits to the Valley. Maybe there was something to Gem's logic. But there was still the matter of the death magic. "Gem," I said softly, all too aware of the time slipping away. "We can't cross to Sanctuary. By the time we did that and then got to Scott in the Valley, it would be too late."

She paled. "What..." Her tongue darted out to moisten her lips. "What are you saying?"

Hands clenched, I looked her in the eye. "I'm saying I need to use death magic to put me straight over to where Scott is."

Gem squeaked and her hand flew to her mouth.

"Please don't stay," I said, lowering my gaze to the ground. "I don't want you to think less of me than you already do." I turned around and waited for the sound of footsteps in the grass.

Two steps, three, four... Then a hand on my shoulder. "Edge," she whispered, then again louder, "Edge. I don't think less of you. I think you're awfully brave. I wish I was half as brave as you."

My throat constricted, but I still didn't turn.

"And I think that you'll have to try a lot harder than that if you don't want me to come with you."

I gave up and turned, searching her eyes for any hint of loathing or falseness. "Really?"

She wound her arm through mine. "Of course."

I could have said more. I could have told her that I didn't *want* her to come with me; that it would be all right; that I didn't need help and I knew what I was doing. All of that could have kept her safe, but it would have been lies. So I said nothing. I just wrapped my arms around her and hugged.

25

"SO, HOW IS this going to work then?" Gem
asked, and to her credit she barely sounded nervous
at all.

I, on the other hand, had to clear my throat twice
before I could get words out. "Um, well, the theory
is that you need to offer a sacrifice, right?" Despite
the time pressing down on us, I didn't want to rush
the explanation. Gem might just spot a flaw I hadn't
thought of that could kill us.

She nodded.

"And it's life or death, and usually seeds or small
animals."

"Yes." She nodded again.

"So I thought..." I cleared my throat. "I thought
that I could probably use myself."

Gem squeaked, but I held up a hand to stop her.
"Look, we're in a huge hurry here, okay. Either this

is going to work and we have a shot at stopping Scott, who is by now at least"—I checked the watch I was wearing while my phone was still in its rice bath—"six minutes ahead of us. Six minutes is an awfully long time when you're as close to going under as he is. He might be gone already. But either this works, and we can try to stop him, or it doesn't work, and I promise you, I will go to Sanctuary the proper way and let the fairies deal with the fallout." I drew an X over my chest. "Cross my heart."

"Or it doesn't work and we die."

I rolled my eyes. "Thank you. I totally hadn't considered that possibility."

Gem sighed reluctantly. "Okay, fine. But... sacrifice yourself? You're not... you're not planning to kill yourself, are you?"

I started. "What? No! Why would you...?" I gave my head a shake to purge the thought. "Never mind. No. Look, the way I see it, it doesn't need to be a complete death in order to work. After all, we're making the seeds grow, but not to full height instantly. There's an initial spurt of growth that provides the power. So it's probably the same with death. There's an initial power surge in the process, and then the power ratio tapers away. Right?"

Gem gave me dubious puppy eyes. "How do you start to die and yet not?"

"Blood," I said simply. I took her hand. "Are you ready?"

She nodded, keeping her distance.

"Good. Hold onto my arm." I drew her close and tucked her hand into the crook of my elbow.

Positioning the sharp rock I'd found in the dirt over the back of one hand, I glanced at her. She stared at the rock, transfixed and pale-faced. "Probably best if you close your eyes," I said. "And if this is anything like the time Scott transported me, it will hurt."

Her jaw tensed, but she closed her eyes.

"Good." I closed mine too and imagined where I wanted to be: in the Valley, right near the sinkhole. Jumping straight into it was an experience I didn't care to repeat, but I'd bet anything in the world that that was where Scott had gone.

I held my breath and tore the rock across my skin. *Ow.* Blood welled, then dripped. I shook my hand gently and blood fell to the ground. I concentrated on the Valley.

For a heartbeat I thought it hadn't worked, then, once again, the world disappeared in mind-bending agony as fire ran through my veins.

Gem stood over me and brushed off her school skirt, the movement making her swirl in a field of bright, swooping lights.

"Well," she said as I clutched at my temples and groaned. "That wasn't as bad as I expected. I'd like to be mad at you for even *thinking* about trying it, but," she looked around, "we're here. So I suppose it's okay." She held out three hands.

I blinked. Two hands. Three. Four. One. Seven? "How many hands do you have?" My voice came out groggy.

Gem knelt in front of me and peered into my eyes. "Oh my gosh. I *knew* it was too good to be true. Are you okay?"

I blinked rapidly, trying to clear the doubles and triples from my vision. "Maybe?" I slurred. "Feel... funny." Without warning I toppled over backwards. I lay still, staring up at the sky, trying to orient myself. Surely the ground wasn't supposed to be whirling underneath me.

Gem exhaled in frustration. "We can't go on like this, Emma. I *knew* this was too dangerous." She tugged on her hair.

"No," I said from my position flat on the ground. "I'm fine. Gimme a second."

Gem's face clouded. She reached out and squeezed my hand. "Hurry."

Nerves squeezed my insides. Scott was probably gone by now, if not completely then at least irreparably. The fairies wouldn't be able to do anything but damage control, and considering they hadn't even been able to stop the shadows from spawning in the first place, I doubted there was much they could do to stop them spreading over Sanctuary, Earth, and wherever else it was that Sanctuary could take them.

I sat unsteadily. "Look, see. Sitting. Ta da!"

Gem snorted. "Hilarious. Are you sure you're okay? We don't have to go, you know."

I crouched awkwardly, head hanging. "Yeah, we kind of do."

Gem nodded and helped me up. "I know. I was just trying to make you feel better."

"I'm good," I said. I wobbled a little as I gained uprightness, but I ignored my whirling head and gave Gem the cheesiest grin I could manage. "See?"

She sighed. "I'm going to ignore the fact that you're about to fall over and just agree, because I know you won't stay here even if I tell you to. So let's go." She began walking, heading straight for the Valley's sinkhole.

"Wait," I said, skipping a couple of steps to catch up and nearly falling onto her shoulder. "How did you know which way to go?"

She did sarcastic jazz hands around her head. "Valley girl, remember?"

I snorted. "Funny."

"I try."

I bumped her hip—or tried to; it turned into more of a stumble. "It's going to be okay," I said. "I mean, maybe not the Scott thing. He could be..." I stopped, unable to voice it aloud. "But anyway, I mean you. The Valley. After this, we'll never have to come here again, and you'll be just fine."

"Assuming the shadows don't take over Earth too, you mean." She shot me a tight smile. "Thanks for trying."

"It's true, Gem," I said. "You're my best friend. I won't let anything happen to you. I promise."

26

MY HEAD CLEARED as we walked, and a minute later we stopped in a fringe of trees, staring down at the sinkhole. It was definitely bigger than before, taking up most of the treeless valley, a swirling mass of dense darkness.

Gemma rubbed at her arms. "That's it?"

I glanced at her. "Yes. Didn't you see it the last time?"

She shook her head. "I don't remember. I don't remember anything except the light, and then I was with Aphros."

I wrinkled my brow. "Yeah, how did she do that, by the way? Did you ever ask her?"

Gem shuddered. "It was..." She licked her lips. "It was because I approached the light. It's the Valley itself, its thoughts and mind, whatever, and because she's both life and death, she can talk to people when they're right in the heart of either Sanctuary or the Valley—or when she is, I guess." She glanced sideways at me. "She must have been in the sinkhole when she grabbed you and dragged you over that first time."

I nodded, remembering how I'd torn her out of it without knowing what I was doing. I shivered as I remembered her voice cutting off, and her frantic command to flee.

"Anyway," Gem continued. "She told me to come with her, but I didn't listen. The light... It showed me things, Edge." She turned to me, eyes wide and pleading. "I saw... what it would be like if..." She swallowed, and I could tell she was fighting a break down.

I hugged her. "Hey, it's okay. I don't need to know what you saw. It showed me things too." I cleared my throat as I recalled the perfect life it had offered. "I just wanted to know what Aphros did."

She drew back and wiped her tears, drawing in a great, shuddery breath. "After I'd said yes to the light, it tried to"—she waved her hands in front of her—"I don't know, absorb me, or something. But Aphros's pillar of light got there first, and it covered me, and I felt like, like, I don't know, like cold was burning through me, but it was refreshing, not painful. And then it stopped, and I was with her."

"Okay," I said. "Let me think a minute before we go in." I chewed on my lip, trying to puzzle it out.

Point one, the pillars of light were soulprints, I was sure of that. I'd seen them too when I'd been in the sinkhole, and they'd set my Road Mastery blaring. And for Gemma to be able to see them without Road Mastery, they had to be strong, really, really strong.

Point two, the unicorn's soulprint could manifest like that in the heart of the Valley, and presumably in the heart of Sanctuary too, if Sanctuary had one, because she was made from life and death magic. So non-magical beings wouldn't have their soulprint show up like that, probably. Interesting.

Point three, Gem had agreed to the light's bargain, and it tried to consume her. Scott had agreed to the bargain too, I was assuming, and now his soulprint was tainted by the Valley's. Had the light tried to swallow him up as well? Was that how he'd been entangled? If so, it meant that while Gem belonged to the Valley (because she'd agreed to its bargain), she also belonged to the unicorn, because Aphros had absorbed Gem into her own soulprint. That definitely bore thinking about. It also meant that her soulprint might become tainted by the Valley's, but that was a problem for later.

I stared at her with my Road Mastery and caught a tiny whiff of mint. "Gem, where's Aphros?" I asked casually.

"Over there," she replied immediately, pointing. "Why's that?"

I shook my head. Interesting. So Gemma was bonded to the Valley, *and* to the unicorn. All we needed to do was bind her to Sanctuary as well, and she'd have the complete set. Ha.

I rubbed my face. My brain was about to start leaking out my ears. So Gemma could sense the unicorn. The unicorn had to stay in the Valley because if she left, there'd be nothing to keep the darkness in check. Which meant the unicorn had some way of keeping it in check. But she needed me—or someone else, anyway—to deal with Scott, because if the Valley got Scott, she wouldn't be able to help.

I really needed to find Scott.

"So what are you thinking?" Gem said at last.

I laid it out for her, including the bit about her being somehow bound to the unicorn, just as Scott was to the Valley.

She blinked at that. "So, what? Aphros will gradually start taking over my body?"

I shook my head. "No. I think the Valley is only doing that to Scott because it doesn't have a body of its own, and it wants one. Aphros... I have no idea. You can tell me where she is without thinking, so there's that, and when I look closely at you I can see traces of her on you. They're faint, not like with the Valley on Scott. He must have been coming here for quite a while to get that entangled. Or maybe it's because the Valley wants his body. I don't know," I concluded. "I'm not sure what it will do. But..." I hesitated, knowing she wasn't going to like this bit.

"What?"

"I don't think it's safe for you to come into the sinkhole," I said in a rush. "I know you said it might be fine, and the Valley might not hurt you because it has some kind of connection with you, but that's part of the point; the longer you spend in there, the stronger that connection will get." I searched her face. "I don't want to lose the best friend I ever had now I've found her again."

Gem crushed me in a hug. "You idiot. You're my best friend too." She took a deep breath. "Okay."

I blinked. "Okay? Okay as in you won't come in with me?"

She rubbed her arms. "I won't pretend I don't want to. I don't think it will hurt me, like I said before. But for one, I trust you and your Road Mastery. And for two..." Her eyes became haunted, and when she continued her voice was hoarse. "I *want* to come in with you. Badly." She hugged herself and goosebumps broke out on her skin. "And if I want this badly to head into the middle of an evil sinkhole of power... Edge, I don't think it's me doing the wanting."

I wrapped my arms around her. "Oh Gem," I whispered into her hair.

We broke apart, both with tears in our eyes, but this time her voice was steady. "And anyway.

Someone has to stick around to tell Sanctuary what happened if it all... You know."

I nodded. "You're the best, Gem."

She tried a smile. "You too. Be careful."

"Promise," I said. "I'll be right back."

27

INSIDE THE SINKHOLE, I looked around, both with my eyes and my Road Mastery. Black everywhere. Sighing, I picked a random direction and walked. Forever later, the scenery changed: a tiny, fleeting flicker of darkness emptier than the rest, howling like wind over bare hilltops. Scott. I altered my course a little to the right and crept toward him. Nerves jangled in my stomach and I eased my feet down. I doubted very much that he was a Road Master, and there was no way he could see me in this darkness, but a stray rustle of my uniform could easily give me away.

I smoothed my hands down my skirt. Frogging elephants. In my school uniform *again*? That was just asking for a grounding, since the one I'd been wearing last time didn't even make it back home— the fairies had burned it as contaminated.

I inched closer—and there was Scott. Around him the darkness had lifted a little, but where it had gone from the air, it had gathered in his eyes, pupils dilating to fill his entire eye space—or else the iris and the whites had turned black. Either way, the effect was horrific. I shuddered.

He turned to me, jet-black orbs piercing and terrifying. "You found me."

I forced my hands to unclench. "Yes."

"Please," he said, smile lean and hungry. "Take a seat." A stool appeared at his gesture, metallic and glimmering, slightly too perfect to be real.

"No thanks." I folded my arms over my chest to stop them trembling.

"Oh, come now, Emma Tanning. You are visiting my home. At least allow me to be hospitable."

Chills ran down my neck. Scott didn't talk like that, and he didn't call me by my full name. I sat, unwilling to anger the Valley's sentient power as it spoke through a boy I'd once known.

My heart pounded. I was too late.

Scott was gone, and now I'd have to fight the power of the Valley itself if I ever wanted to get out of here alive. I closed my eyes—and the wind swept toward me over mountaintops.

It was faint, but there was no mistaking Scott's soulprint. Surely he had to be in there somewhere if I could still sense that.

"There. Isn't that better?"

I nodded.

"Lovely." Scott sat on a matching stool that appeared under him right as he landed on it. "So. I'd like to have a talk with you, if I may."

If I may? Seriously? And it didn't think I'd notice that it wasn't Scott talking? Then again, maybe it didn't care. My fingers twitched. "Sure."

He leaned back, crossing his ankles. "What do you know about the shadows?"

My eyebrows lifted. "The shadows?" Not the first thing I thought it would ask, that's for sure. "Um, they're a product of death magic, something to do with the Valley's power. They're leaking over at the crossing points between worlds, and things are being snatched into them." Including Gemma. And Veve. More chills chased down my spine.

"Half right," Scott's body replied. "They are indeed a product of 'death magic', as you so belittlingly call it, and I see how you might call it leaking. Things are not, however, being snatched. They were called, by me as I tested the limits of my newfound power and sought to expand them."

I stiffened and my hands fisted. "Called? How about stolen? Kidnapped, even. I'm pretty sure Gemma didn't hear your voice and come running."

The Valley-Scott laughed. "Ah, my ignorant Princess."

Ice spiked through my veins. How dare it use that name? How *dare* it!

"All you know about death magic, you have been told from liars. Tell me, what do you think of death magic, Emma Tanning? Tell me truly, now that you have felt its power yourself."

My throat went dry. "I haven't..." I stammered. "I mean I..." I scrubbed my hands on my skirt, leaving trails of sweat.

Valley-Scott laughed again. "You see? I know everything. I even know where your friends are— the annoying green one, who I will soon be able to destroy once and for all, and the one like the night sky who forsook you."

I half stood before I remembered that attacking the heart of the Valley outright might not be such a good plan. *She did not forsake me.* My fingernails bit into my palms. "You *tricked* her."

He scoffed. "I tricked no one. I made the terms of my bargain clear."

"Oh? Like you made them clear for me? Here, Emma, have all this power and you can protect your family; here, Emma, create a perfect life for yourself using death; oh, but Emma, I won't tell you that I'll *devour your soul* if you do." I glared at him. "Seriously?"

Valley-Scott narrowed his eyes at me. "You tread close to danger, girl."

"Really? And here I thought this was a picnic."

"Enough!" Valley-Scott stood up, black eyes gleaming. "You have been told my magic is filth, that it corrupts your soul and destroys the balance. But it was the fairies that told you this, and they are creatures of Sanctuary. Not one of them has ever set foot in the Valley, because if they did, they would cease to exist." He loomed over me. "And yet you would trust their opinion on the sacrifice?"

I opened my mouth to retort that yes, actually, I did—only he had a point. The fairies were suspiciously close-mouthed about a lot of things, come to think of it, and Quoise had even admitted that helping me could get her into huge trouble. But all I'd been doing was rescuing people from the shadows, from the Valley—the death magic they were supposed to be against.

Valley-Scott looked smug. "You see? Even you, with your charmingly inflexible opinions on morals, find them untrustworthy."

My head was whirling. This was too much. It was *all* too much. I'd used death magic to make a crossing, and while I'd felt sick afterwards, there didn't seem to be any lasting damage done.

Either the fairies were lying, or it was a cumulative thing, something that built up the more you used the magic, like, like plaque—or like Scott and Gemma slowly falling under the influence of the Valley.

That shook me free of my spinning doubts. "No," I said, standing up. "You are not going to get to me like this."

Darkness flared around us. "Why, whatever do you mean?" His voice snaked around me as he crooned. "I'm just trying to show you the truth."

I shut my eyes. "No, you're not. Even if the fairies are hiding things, or are biased, or whatever, it doesn't mean you're telling the truth. I don't believe you, I don't accept anything you have to offer, and I deny your power over me!" I'd started out talking normally but by the end of my speech I was shouting. "Keep away from me!"

Valley-Scott raised his hand, ready to strike. I felt him tense for the blow, saw his hand approaching.

I caught it. "No. You will not use that body against me any more."

I laid my free hand against Scott's cheek and, heedless of the dark that boiled around us, leaned my forehead against his.

"Scott," I said desperately. "I know you're still in there somewhere, I can sense you. I don't know if you can hear me, but if you can, please listen. I don't like you. I think you're a jerk, actually. But I'm willing to concede that at least a little bit of that might be the Valley's power acting through you, and although I still think you're a stupid idiot for getting yourself tangled up in all this, I'll make you a deal: resist him now, and we can start over.

"I'm not promising you anything, not even the tiniest bit of anything—all I'm saying is, if you help me now, just this once, to beat the darkness, then you'll have a clean slate with me, okay? From there, it's up to you."

Come on, I thought desperately. I closed my eyes against the warmth of his forehead and strained with all the Road Mastery I had. *Come on, Scott. I know you're in there. Listen to me!* I grasped at the faint breeze, the sense of wide-open spaces. *Come on!*

My hand was slipping from around his wrist. Any moment now I'd lose my grip and he'd punch me, and that would be the beginning of the end.

"Come on, Scott," I murmured. "Come on."

His cheek twitched under my palm. The wind gusted once and vanished. He strained against me harder, and I could barely keep his fist from grazing my chin. My fingers ached.

Please! Scott! Come on!

I couldn't hold him. His wrist slipped from my grip and I cried out, bracing for the blow. "Scott! Please!"

The sense of wind across a night time hilltop strengthened and at the last moment, Scott's body crumbled. He collapsed to the ground, almost dragging me down.

I fought to catch him, snatching after the last whisper of his soulprint with my Road Mastery. *Oh no you don't.* I wrenched after his soulprint, feeling like I was split in two as I tried to hold onto both it and him. Slowly, slowly, I hauled the soulprint back toward us and stuffed it into his body.

He gasped. "Emma." He clung to me, unable to bear his own weight, head against my stomach.

My heart just about stopped. He'd done it. I'd done it. We'd broken the Valley's hold on him and for just a moment, the darkness retreated.

I drew Scott upright and he hung around my neck, burying his face into my shoulder and sobbing. I stood stunned for a moment, arms awkward, then sighed. I hugged him, patting his back with one hand. He was a complete cretin, and I didn't like him one iota more than I'd ever done, but I'd promised him a clean slate. Right now, he was just a terrified kid having a break down.

Something pointy poked me in the hip. I shifted, and the pointy thing fell out of Scott's pocket and clunked on the ground. I twisted down and snagged it, holding it up over Scott's shoulder so I could examine it.

I nearly dropped it again when I saw it was the clockwork fairy he'd set on me last time. I turned it over. It might have been an instrument of evil, but it sure was well made. Not a blemish on her.

...Except a small mark on her shoulder. I brought it closer and squinted.

The fairy clattered to the ground a second time.

I swallowed hard and forced myself to breathe. Her shoulder had read, *For the Princess*.

28

MY HEART POUNDED, but the clatter of the fairy barely had time to die away before something crackled and fizzled over my shoulder. Scott jerked upright and stared open-mouthed, fingers digging into my back. I pried him loose and turned, stomach heavy with dread.

The pillar of light. It snapped and popped like electricity, and before I could react, lightning shot out of it. Scott crumpled to the ground. I screamed.

I crouched over him and felt for a pulse in his neck, my own pounding. He was *not* going to die now, not right after I'd given him a clean slate. He was going to have a chance to be a decent human being, he *was*.

A pulse fluttered under my fingertips, weak and erratic, but there.

I drew myself up and faced the light, shielding him behind me. "What was that for?"

"He is no use to me any longer," the light said. "If he will not submit, he will die."

"And you're trying to convince me that you're the *good* side?" I threw my hands up. "You're disgusting!" *Not to mention cold, calculating, ruthless, and evil, but hey, let's not get carried away here.*

The light flashed within arm's reach. "My offer to you still stands," it crooned. "The power to change the world, Emma Tanning. It needn't all be bad. You could do whatever you wanted. All I ask is a body to share, that I might walk the worlds and see for myself the things that I have heard."

Anger bubbled in my chest. "First of all, I'm not agreeing to *anything* you have to offer. I wouldn't have *any* power, because you're stronger than me, and the only thing you want me for is my body. Second of all, why do you even *want* a body? I mean, not why," I corrected myself as things clicked into place. "How. *How* can you want a body. Because you're..." I waved my hands. "You're a place. A thing. You shouldn't want anything at all."

The light licked around me, closer and closer. "Because I live." Intense hunger filled its voice. "And I desire only what all living things desire: life. More life. More, always more."

I stiffened as a tendril of blackness swept across my arm. The touch was feather-light on my skin, but weighed heavier than the world on my Road Mastery. Fear thrilled through me. It was true. The Valley was stronger than me, so terribly, fearfully strong. I wasn't going to make it out of here alive. Aphros had said that I had to separate Scott from the Valley; she hadn't mentioned anything about having to fight the Valley afterwards.

Maybe she hadn't meant me to. Maybe she'd known I would die here, and didn't care. She was part death, after all.

"Do not judge me for desiring only what we all desire, Emma Tanning. Especially when I know that you too desire life."

Images forced their way into my mind, images of greatness and adoration. I shoved them down.

Aphros had saved Gem. She stayed in the Valley because she was holding it in check. And she could manifest her own life force here in the heart of the Valley. She couldn't be evil.

Aphros? I thought it as loudly as I could, reaching out with my Road Mastery. *Are you there? Can you hear me? I need your help.*

A breath of wind touched my face—mint.

Please, I said quickly. *You have to come. I've got Scott and he's okay, except he's unconscious, and the light, the Valley is here, and I can't fight it, it's too big, too strong. I don't know what to do.*

The light crackled louder. "What are you doing? To whom are you speaking?"

"None of your business," I snapped. "And besides, you still didn't answer my question. You're a place. A thing. *How are you alive?*"

Aphros's answer came. *It is too strong. Too alive. It has taken on too much of the boy and I cannot stop it.*

I covered my face. I'd been too slow. I'd saved Scott, but it had been too late after all. *Please, Aphros. Please, you have to try!*

The light popped and crackled. "The boy gave me life," it said. "Together, we were stronger than we could ever be alone."

It continued, but I'd frozen in place. Stronger together than alone.

Aphros, I sent urgently. *You can manifest your soulprint here, can't you?*

Yes.

"Answer me!" The light darted around me, touching bare skin at my knees, elbows, neck.

I gasped as deathly cold stole air from my lungs. Gulping, I scrunched my eyes closed. *If I were to step into your soulprint, what would happen?*

The same as for the girl, Gem. Her thoughts sharpened. *We would become one for an instant. I could draw you to me, if you wanted.*

My heart pounded. *Only an instant?*

I am not like the Valley. I have no need for a body that is not mine. Her thoughts dripped with loathing.

"Emma Tanning, I command you now: speak! Answer me, or you shall die!"

Air squeezed from my lungs. I gasped again. It hurt, burning like ice. I had no breath to answer, even if I'd heard the light's question.

I shoved the pain aside, locking it away in the edges of my mind. *So what would happen?*

A connection would form. A bond.

Any second now, my heart would break out of my chest. *Could we beat the Valley together?*

Silence, in which my senses numbed as my body began to fail. But then, *Yes*.

Green light flared, a twisting, spiralling pillar almost as large as the Valley's. I heaved with everything I had, lights of exertion popping in my eyes, and threw myself sideways. Cold like an icy shower in midsummer gripped me and was gone, and with it went the pain. I sucked in air and stood.

The Valley light howled in anger. "You will not take another from me! You will not!" It lashed toward me.

I ducked, but the light grazed against my head. It hurt, a blinding agony that stole all thought for just an instant.

Scott's body began to rise slowly from the ground.

I threw myself at him. "Leave! Him! Alone!"

Darkness snaked up out of his body and wrapped around me. I fought and struggled, but it wound tighter until it engulfed me, binding me to Scott's body, and I saw the part of it that had come from him, the part of it that was alive—hatred and anger and fear so human I reeled.

We can separate them, Aphros said. *Pull it out as you pulled me. But you must destroy the human part; I cannot touch it.*

Wind roared in my ears I called up my Road Mastery more deeply than I ever had before and threw it wide. The unicorn's power amplified it, stretching and moulding it to a knife's edge. I swung it down and cleaved the darkness in two, and as the lighter side fell away I drew myself up to face the remainder.

"No!" it shrieked. "I will not go! I will not be reduced!"

I stretched out through the storm that raged around us and took the darkness in my fist. I squeezed. It writhed and shrieked. My hand burned, fire and agony white hot against the black, and I screamed as I crushed the darkness into nothing.

It gave one last anguished howl, and vanished.

My hand and chest burned. I staggered, Scott's full weight suddenly in my arms, and we dropped to the ground. The darkness had shredded; light shot through the gaps, illuminating the area like sunrise after rain, and the last of the black mist began to evaporate.

You have done well, Aphros sent on a sunbeam. *It is over.* The weight of her presence lifted from my chest, and gaspingly, I could breathe.

29

THE REMAINING SHADOWS drained slowly away, taking with them the rancid smell that would forever be linked to the Valley in my mind. All around, the trees began to lift, branches righting themselves, leaves regaining their colour. Even the grass seemed less downtrodden.

And there, up in the tree line, a glimmer of midnight blue and diamonds; the smell of mint and gold. Grinning madly, chest lighter than air, I ran over to them. Gemma untangled her fingers from Aphros's mane and flung herself at me. "I knew you'd come."

"Are you okay?" I asked, crushing her in return with my burned hand held awkwardly to one side.

"I'm fine!"

I laughed, the sound of relief bursting up through fear. "Then come on! Let's go home."

Together we loaded Scott onto Aphros's back and climbed aboard ourselves. Of course, Gemma made me sit in front, so I had an unconscious Scott draped over my thighs. But I was still sky high from crushing the darkness; a little thing like Scott on my lap wasn't going to ruin it for me. And *he* never needed to know what had happened.

I laughed at that. It was over. We'd won.

Gem hugged me from behind. "I'm so glad you're my friend."

I tilted my head toward her. "Me too."

"I don't know about you, but I plan to get home and sleep for forty-eight hours." She grinned.

"Forty-eight?" I joked. "I'm sleeping for a week."

Gem laughed. "Maybe a month. A month could be good." A second later she piped up again. "What about May?"

"What about it?"

"All the assessment in the world is due in May. Can we sleep past that, do you think?"

I smothered a giggle. "Sure. Why not?"

At full speed, it only took Aphros twenty minutes to reach the border of Sanctuary. She leapt over the boundary at a canter, continuing up through the promenade of trees and on to the main entrance hall via the wide, airy passage Quoise had showed me. Fairies scattered left and right as she cantered through, all of them shouting excitedly as they realised it was Aphros.

We continued straight out of the lodge and down to the stables. Of course. The unicorn twins.

Aphros paused outside the stables to let us off, but before she could enter, Quoise burst from the doorway, followed by Mrs Caro and—

"*Mum?*"

"Emma!"

Our respective mothers swept us up into hugs before I could even process the fact that my mother was in Sanctuary. There were frantic explanations on both sides—the school had called them in a frenzy because we'd gone missing, and Mrs Caro had guessed what had happened. She'd called Mum, told her she knew where we were and that we were in danger, and asked her to come to the clearing. She'd given a quick explanation and before Mum could protest disbelief, Mrs Caro had brought her over to Sanctuary.

On our side, we explained why we'd ditched school and gone back to the Valley despite our promises not to—and why we had an unconscious schoolboy on a unicorn with us.

Quoise took one look at Scott and flew straight up toward the Lodge, no doubt seeking medical assistance.

Aphros reappeared at the stable door. I ran to her, beaming. The fingers of my good hand tangled through her mane and she hooked me closer with her nose. "Are they okay?" I asked.

"Never better."

I hugged her tight. "I... I just have one quick question."

"Ask."

I bit my lip, then tumbled the question out in a rush. "Am I going to become evil because I used death magic?"

She snorted, a sound that echoed with laughter in my head. "I am made of so-called death magic, as I am made of life. Am I evil?"

"Of course not." *Of course not!* I squeezed her tight. "Thank you, Aphros," I murmured into her neck. "Thank you."

"Thank *you*." She stepped away. I straightened and watched as she went to Gem. I'd nearly forgotten that Gem was bound to Aphros too. They talked quietly for a moment, then one of the unicorn foals whinnied. Aphros untangled herself from Gem's hug and hurried back inside.

Mum swept me up from behind in a bone-crushing hug. I fought for air, but I wasn't going to tell her to stop. Instead, I let her usher me to the alcove, with her proclaiming that I'd have dinner when I got home, whatever I wanted to eat, and a hot bath with the fancy bath salts, and I could sleep for the rest of the week if I wanted to.

Mm. Bed. I gave Sanctuary a last look: its lush, emerald grass and perfect dusk sky, the only shadows normal and harmless. Safe. *Home.*

"What's wrong?" Mum asked, because I'd stopped, and I shook my head and kept walking.

"Nothing," I said. "Nothing's wrong at all." Because then we crossed back to Earth and we came out in the clearing, and as I looked around and saw that the shadows there were normal too, it also felt like home.

And I had two of them.

And they were both safe.

And no one would take them away.

"I love you, Mum," I said.

"I love you too, Em." She squeezed my hand as we climbed the steps through the granite boulders that led up to our street. She opened the back gate for me, pushing a bouncing Veve aside. "I'm proud of you, Emma," she said. "Welcome home."

THANK YOU!

Dear You,

Thank you for taking the time to read this book! I hope you enjoyed reading it as much as I enjoyed making it. Actually, I hope you enjoyed it more, because editing this book was pretty hard, and I'd hate for it to have been that hard to read. So: I hope you enjoyed reading this book, like, A LOT. There.

If you *did* like it, and you'd like to see more *Sanctuary* books, please consider leaving a review wherever you bought this book, or on Amazon, or GoodReads, or on your school or work noticeboard, or scrawled on your best friend's hand. Probably not their face. That would be a little cruel. But anywhere else works, really. It's the fact that you recommended it to someone that matters.

(Also don't use blood. You don't want to end up in the Valley, do you? No. I didn't think so.)

Anyway, if you made it this far, you are genuinely amazing, and I love and adore you. YOU are what makes writing books worthwhile. Thank you :3

Love and unicorns,
Amy

ACKNOWLEDGEMENTS

Do you have any idea how many people it takes to make a good book? I didn't, until I started trying to write them. Here are the incredible people that THIS book wouldn't have existed without, in order of how I drew them out of a hat*:

Merc Rustad and Ada Hoffmann, for encouragement through the very first drafts. This book would literally not have been written without you two cheering me along, so THANKS. You two are awesome.

Renn Hadley, Lauren Orbison, Kerryn Frampton, Michelle D. Argyle, Emily Casey, Anna Humphrey and Stephanie McGee—you guys were a SUPER team of beta readers when I needed you most. Thanks for helping me figure out the genre of this beast and tidy it up.
(Especially Steph for spotting the magic dog lead!)

Belynda Lomas deserves special thanks for helping me do the actual physical work of editing—I don't know how many hundreds of corrections you typed in to help me hit that deadline, but whoa, thank you.

The Pitch Wars mentors who gave me feedback on my first fifty pages also deserve immense thanks: J.C. Davis, Wade White, Catherine Scully and Juliana Brandt. Your time and words were greatly appreciated.

Finally, my God and my family (especially Daimien, who always believes in me, and Carol, who loved this story first)—thank you.

*Lies, all lies.

ABOUT THE AUTHOR

AMY LAURENS is an Australian author of fantasy fiction for all ages. She has never seen a fairy or travelled to Sanctuary (sadly), but she has definitely owned a Labrador almost exactly like Veve (though Amy's Labrador was yellow, not brown).

And while she's definitely not a Road Master (pity), her kids are pretty sure she has eyes in the back of her head and a sixth sense for spotting trouble. She hasn't told anyone this, but actually she has *two* sets of eyes in the back of her head— one because she's a mum, and one because she's a teacher.

You can find out more about Amy at her website, www.amylaurens.com.

1

SOMEONE TAPPED LIGHTLY on my bedroom door. Groggy with sleep, I felt about in the dark for my phone. The lock screen told me it was nearly 2am. My pulse kicked. It had to be about Gemma, my best friend. My *sick* best friend. "Come in," I said hoarsely.

Mum crept in, house phone in hand.

"Is Gemma okay?" I asked before she spoke.

"I understand," she said, and it took me a second to realise that she was talking to the phone. She hung up and sat on my bed.

I shifted my legs out of the way and waited, barely breathing. The darkness pressed in around us, heavy, full of secrets and fears.

"Is it really something only you can fix?" she asked me. In the shadows, I watched as she twisted the phone in her hands.

I wriggled over and lay my head against her hip, revealing in the comfort of her choc-chip-cookies-and-steel soulprint—the unique sensory aura that all people had, and that I could sense and sometimes manipulate because I was a Road Master. "I don't know if I can fix it," I said truthfully. "But I know the doctors can't. She'll die no matter what they do." My pulse stuttered again. Gemma wasn't going to die. I wouldn't let her. "I need to get her to Sanctuary, I think," I said, referring to the home of the fairies that Gemma and I had the ability to travel to.

Unfortunately, Sanctuary wasn't the only other world in existence. The Valley, known more properly as the Valley of Death, was Sanctuary's opposite; where Sanctuary was based on life magic, the Valley ran on death.

And now it had its shadowy tendrils wrapped firmly around my best friend.

In the waiting night, I pressed my eyes shut, trying to remember exactly what the Valley's connection to Gem had looked like. More or less like Scott? Less. Definitely less.

"And Gemma can't just go there by herself?"

"Mum." I shook my head. "She's sick. Like, really sick. Keep her in the hospital overnight sick, remember?"

Mum shot me a sideways glance that I could read more from the slight shift of her head than any ability to see her eyes in this light. "No need to sass me, Emma Tanning. You have to understand how absurd this all is from the outside. If it wasn't for Mrs Caro, or..."

I wondered if she was remembering her brief visit to Sanctuary a couple of weeks ago. I shifted awkwardly. "But you've seen it. You know it's real."

She sighed. "You're sure it's something... magical? That's wrong with her?"

I sniffed. "Of course I'm sure. What did Mrs Caro say?"

"That the doctors can't find anything."

"Exactly. 'Soul being drained by Valley of Death' isn't exactly in the medical textbooks, is it?"

Mum hugged me tight. I squirmed until I could breathe. "Be careful, Edge," Mum told me, giving me one last squeeze.

"Always."

The house creaked in the darkness around us, finally cooling after another hot, summery day.

"Liv?" The door protested briefly as Dad nudged it open.

Cool air from the lounge room aircon unit followed him in, chilling my arms.

"What's wrong?" he murmured.

"It's Gemma," Mum said softly. "She's getting worse. Maria says they need Emma. To... help."

Help. I had to help her. I'd fixed Scott; surely I could save my best friend too.

"I'm going to drive Emma down now," Mum said as I wriggled out from the covers and crossed the night-still bedroom to find clothes.

"Do you want me to come?" Dad asked.

"It's fine," Mum said. "You have meetings tomorrow. I can stay home if I need to."

I couldn't, though, I thought as I pulled on my jeans. No matter what happened tonight, there was no way I was missing school tomorrow. A certain teenage boy held answers to some very important questions, and I'd get those answers or die trying. He wouldn't even know what hit him.

"I'm ready," I said, interrupting Dad as I straightened out my shirt.

Mum stood, the bed pinging and creaking as she did. "Let me get dressed too."

I waited in the front hallway. Tree shadows rippled through the narrow windows on either side of the door reaching across the floor tiles, rustling, straining. I stood where they ended and watched as my toes dipped in and out of darkness.

In and out, in and out. Dark and light, dark and light.

One step in either direction and I could be safe, or drown forever.

"Ready?" Mum said behind me, keys clinking too loudly in the night.

I stepped to the front door, into the shadows. "Ready." *I'm coming, Gemma,* I told her. *I'm coming.*